To Carol from Allene
Feb.. 2007

D0462844

Buster's Diaries

Buster's Diaries

A TRUE STORY OF A DOG AND HIS MAN
AS TOLD TO ROY HATTERSLEY

WARNER BOOKS

A Time Warner Company

Warner Books, Inc., 1271 Avenue of the Americas, New York, NY 10020
Visit our Web site at www.twbookmark.com

 A Time Warner Company

Printed in the United States of America
First U.S. Printing: October 2000

10 9 8 7 6 5 4 3 2 1

Library of Congress Cataloging-in-Publication Data

Hattersley, Roy.
  Buster's diaries : the true stroy of a dog and his man / by Roy Hattersley.
    p.   cm.
  ISBN 0-446-52662-2
    1. Buster (Dog)--Fiction 2. Dogs--Fiction. 3. Human-animal
relationships. 4. London (England)--Fiction. I Title.

PR6058.A83 B87 2000
823'.914--dc21   00-039896

Introduction

My brother and I were born in the overgrown back garden of a house in Paddington, London, sometime during February 1995. When we were a few days old, our mother was bitten by a rat and the man who owned her tied her to a fence post and left her to die. For nearly a week, she survived on water which was leaking from a hose, and she fed us till she died. Then Diana, the lady who lived next door, rescued us. Being too young and stupid to recognize kindness, after a couple of weeks we ran away and started to live rough. It was the beginning of my fascination with garbage. Even now, with two square meals a day and more biscuits than are good for me, I find black bags and garbage cans irresistible.

We had been vagrants for more than two months when Doris Turner saw us running about on Paddington Recreation Ground. Doris ran the Brent Animal Shelter and decided at once that she must find us a good home. Even then, for reasons I can't explain, I longed for human company. So when Doris called to us, I let her catch me. My brother, being still stupid, ran away again. It was the last time I saw him. Doris said he was my identical twin. Somewhere in North London there is another dog who looks just like me—with the handsome profile of a small Alsatian and the elegant brown-and-gold flecked coat of a Staffordshire bullterrier.

Doris was the first person who ever talked to me. Often I could not understand what she tried to say. But despite that, I liked to listen to the noise she made. Now I understand much more—although I still have difficulty with complicated sentences, especially if they are spoken in a conversational tone. I have a particular problem with subjunctives. But whenever someone speaks to me, I feel happy. Conversation was, I suppose, the beginning of my corruption—or domestication, as humans call it.

Talk is now the noise I hear most often. Because of

that, the wolf within me sleeps—although he sometimes dreams. It was the wolf who kept me alive on the Paddington Recreation Ground, but when he dreams, we go back together to the Siberian forest, not to north London. These days I would not swap my bed against the radiator for a patch of frozen moss under a stunted tree. But I am glad that the wolf is still there, snoring away inside me.

When Doris found me, the wolf was still wide awake and I had not yet learnt that a dog has to choose between the luxury of family life and the excitement of the wild. So I expected to live with Doris for ever, listening to her talk when the mood took me and fighting for my life the rest of the time. But Doris, who was old, thought I needed more exercise than she could organize. So she found me a foster home in a flat a couple of roads away from her house. My new owners did their best to burn off my energy. But I didn't settle down. Sheila—a "home-checker" for the RSPCA and Battersea Dogs' Home—said I "lacked socialization skills with both dogs and humans." I was taken into canine care. Doris and her friends paid the fees.

The people who ran the dogs' home kept me warm and well fed. But they did not talk to me. Indeed, they did not talk to any of the dogs. That was not so bad for the others. They were only there for a week or two while their owners were on holiday. But I thought I would be there for ever. I lost my appetite and my ribs began to show. Even today, if I think I am going to be left alone, I cannot concentrate on my breakfast.

Hoping somebody would adopt me, my beneficiaries put an advertisement in a dog magazine. It said I was "very clean." That was true. It was also insulting. There are much better things to say about me than that. A lady in Gloucester who liked bullterrier crossbreeds wrote to say she might adopt me. But when she saw my picture, I was so thin that she thought I was ill. You have to be a saint to adopt a sick dog.

After a while, I was moved to another kennel in Surrey, where a family kept me—and several other dogs—for more or less nothing. The owners took a special liking to me, perhaps because they were sorry I was so thin or perhaps because they realized what a great dog I would become if someone gave me loving care. They fed me special treats and talked to me a lot. The other dogs did not like me being the favorite. But the wolf inside me kept them in their proper place. I began to grow and put on weight. In fact, I became too healthy for my own good.

I was a victim of the Dangerous Dogs Act. Families which might have adopted me were afraid I would grow into a pit bull terrier, one of the dogs that policemen can take away and shoot. So I stayed at the Surrey kennel for months. Doris died. And I do not know what would have happened to me had Doris's friends not decided on one last advertisement.

Dogs are not supposed to be given as presents. We are for life, not Christmas. But She came to see me at the Surrey orphanage and decided I was "a dog that a Yorkshireman would be proud to own." The Man—who comes from Yorkshire—was not sure he wanted to own any dog at all. He now denies it. But I happen to know that I spent two unnecessary extra weeks in Surrey while he argued about the problems of keeping a dog in London and worried what would happen when he wanted to go to Italy for his holidays. The solution to the second problem was, of course, perfectly simple. He doesn't go to Italy any more.

However, the Man is not as stupid as his first reaction suggests. One day She brought me home. And as soon as he saw me, he knew he wanted to keep me for

7

ever. I was already asleep, but he knelt down by the side of my bed and rubbed me behind the ears. He does that a lot. It is one of his signs of affection. So I enjoy it whether my ears are itching or not. At first, I was not sure how we would get on. I had not even begun to wrestle with the dilemma that all young dogs must face—the choice between independence and comfort. The diary is an account of how I have balanced (not always with complete success) instinct and expediency, self-respect and regular meals, independence and somebody's voice to listen to when I feel sad or lonely.

Over the two years the Man and I have become friends. That is why I accept, with good grace, his disruptive habits and stood by him when he was prosecuted after the incident with the greylag goose in St. James's Park. Until that day in the spring of 1996, I had taken it for granted that we would live for ever in peaceful obscurity. The goose changed all that. I have become public property. Even today, the *Evening Standard* Londoner's Diary telephoned to ask if I had been nominated for one of the "Dogs' Oscars" and expressed bogus incredulity when told that I was waiting for the Whitbread Prize for Literature for my autobiography.

Introduction

There have, I admit, been moments when I have enjoyed my fame. I took especial pleasure in the occasion when he was accosted in the street by a lady who told him, "I know what the dog is called, but I can't remember your name." But sometimes the newspapers have gone too far. I would have tolerated their constant intrusion had they told the consistent truth. But they have changed me from a dog into a brindle cliché. I want people to know what really happens as man and dog learn to live together by gradually accepting each other's limitations and acquiring each other's characteristics. There is more to life than chasing postmen.

Other dogs may resent so intimate a description of the historic battle to reconcile pride in our nature with the comforts of human civilization. To those whom I have offended, I offer my apologies and I express my profound gratitude to the Man for his assistance in putting my diary on paper—though I think he may have invented one or two stories to make it more interesting. Anyway, most of it is true. My earnest wish is that, by working with me on my diaries, he will have found some compensation for his own literary disappointments. These days his frustration is most frequently demonstrated by the constant repetition of third-rate poetry. In our early days he was—insensitively, you may think—particularly addicted to a line from Oliver Goldsmith: "Puppy, mongrel, whelp and hound and cur of low degree." I have learnt to live with such indignities.

I hope that my story will be an inspiration to young dogs everywhere. Do not think of it as a bark-and-tell exposé. It is the account of an odyssey which took a crossbreed orphan from living rough in a public park to the comfort and security of South West London. Within a year of leaving the dogs' orphanage, I was accused (in the *Daily Telegraph*) of being so middle class that I slept on a bean bag. It was not true. But the accusation—by its source and its nature—illustrates how far and how fast I have traveled. I hope you will enjoy my account of the journey.

PART I

Deliverance

In which Buster, a dog of spirit and fortitude, is saved from a life
of want and degradation, and begins to experience both the
penalties and the privileges of domestication.

December 17, 1995—London

I think I shall like it here. There are no other dogs, but there is a Man who would like to be one. When I arrived he got down on his hands and knees, and although he told me to stop licking his face, I knew he didn't mean it. Tomorrow I shall try chewing his ear. Thanks to my dominant personality and animal cunning, I may well become leader of this pack. And even if I don't, there will be real human beings to talk to me.

Everybody was very good about the vomit. The Man helped clean out the animal ambulance (a broken-down old van) and told the driver that I must suffer from motion sickness as I didn't seem to be the nervous type. To be honest, I was terrified. Nobody had told me where I was going or what sort of people were going to look after me. Although I look like one of those fighting dogs in the Sunday newspapers' color magazines, I often feel very insecure. I certainly don't see myself doing ten rounds with a rottweiler. Whenever a skinhead came into the dogs' home, I sat at the back of my kennel and tried to look like a Pekinese.

The dogs' home sent the Man my blue plastic bed—which was wrong, since it gave a false impression. I am absolutely house-trained. The Man had a new bed ready for me. It is woolly with fake sheepskin on the bottom and there is a tartan rug spread over it. I got in straight away. The only thing wrong with the bed is that it has no smell. I shall put that right in the next day or two.

The Man is very inconsistent—the very worst thing possible if he wants a proper relationship with me. As soon as I curled up in a ball, he forgot all about me looking tough and self-confident and said, "He really looks a friendly little chap. I can't believe that anyone was frightened of adopting him. He doesn't look a bit fierce." I almost bit him there and then. I look very fierce indeed standing up—especially when my mouth is open. He will find out in the morning.

He is the talkative type, which is exactly what I wanted. Before I went to sleep he told me that he's signed a form promising not to tie me up, lock me out or give me away. If I behave badly and he doesn't want me any more, I have to go back to the dogs' home. Assuming the food is OK, I shall make myself irresistible. It will not be difficult.

December 18, 1995

The Man has decided that I shall be called Buster. That was not my name before I came to live with him. But since I cannot remember what my old name was, the change does not matter. The Man says my old name made me sound like a hairdresser who is engaged to a second-division soccer player. I think he is a bit of a snob. So am I. At least we have something in common.

I think he must have been sorry he was rude about second-division soccer players' wives. For he began to invent other reasons for calling me Buster. The Man says that I have an optimistic walk, cheerful ears and that my bottom sways with self-confidence. I have no idea what he is talking about. I doubt if even humans understand that sort of nonsense. Still, if he sticks to the one name, I shall soon begin to come when he calls.

December 20, 1995

The food is the same as I got at the dogs' home. It looks like little balls of sawdust. The Man is not allowed to give me my food. When She measures it out, She uses a little glass with lines round the side to make sure I don't get too much. She does not measure out his food. He keeps saying how good it is for me to eat healthy food—usually whilst he is eating chocolate cookies.

I do get "treats." They are dog biscuits, desiccated pigs' ears, rolled, knotted and braided pieces of hide.

There are special rituals associated with treats. Before I get a pig's ear, I have to bark very loudly and he has to say, "For God's sake quieten down." I get a biscuit after he tells me, "Sit! . . . Down!" or "Stay!" or "Wait!" My part in the strange ceremony—which takes place about once every ten minutes—is just doing what he suggests. The ceremony is called "training." He read about it in a book he got from the pet shop.

The book explained that dogs are pack animals and that he must not let me be leader. He must never allow me to go first through a door, always move me out of the way rather than step over me, and stop me from jumping on his knee unless he invites me up. The book says it is easy for the Man to stop me being leader of the pack if only he makes clear who is boss.

I don't want him to make clear who is boss. It is bad enough when he just tries. For example, he totally misunderstands chewing. It is a sign of affection from one pack member to another. But as soon as my molars touch his hand he shouts, "Stop! Stop! Stop! Nobody likes teeth except Buster." I like them a lot. If we had the relationship of equals, he would chew me back.

December 25, 1995

There were so many people in the house that nobody took any interest in me. They all said, "Hello, Buster," and one or two patted me on the head. But for most of the time, I was completely ignored—except when I tried to share the potato crisps and little cookies that everybody else was eating. The Man said that if I howled I would go outside into the hall.

I did not mean to spill the whole plate of little sausages all over the floor. All I wanted to do was have a close smell of them and, perhaps, steal one when nobody was looking. The Man said he was less worried about the marks on the carpet than the risk of me choking on one of the little sticks that were stuck into the sausages. But he still put me outside in the hall. I howled.

After I had howled for about an hour, they all moved into the dining room. Hundreds of dishes of food had to be carried from the kitchen along the hall so, naturally enough, I was able to barge my way in when the door was left open. The Man said I would lie quietly on his feet and promised not to feed me bits of turkey. Because he kept his promise, I did not lie quietly at his feet. When I stood on my hind legs and put my feet on the table, I was put out into the hall again. I howled.

When the people went home, they all said how much they had enjoyed themselves. I did not enjoy myself. Before they left, I was shut in the kitchen, with all the food locked away in cupboards. When he took me for my late-night walk, the Man said, "Buster, you're stupid. If you'd been well behaved, you could have stayed with me and picked up the food I dropped." I don't know if he meant dropped by mistake or dropped specially for me.

I shall think about what he said. Being well behaved when there are strange people about is more difficult than he thinks—especially if some of them smell of fear. But I would have liked the dropped food. Today was a Christmas. If there is another one next week, I shall try to make the best of it.

December 29, 1995

I think the Man must be a slow learner. She picked up the idea in a couple of weeks. Calm voice. Authoritative tone. Firm information. Whenever he rebukes me, he either shouts or giggles, which is very bad. Sometimes he does both at the same time, which is even worse. Then, even if I haven't quite done what he tells me, he gives me a hug. If we go on in this way, I shall never learn how to behave.

I am beginning to learn about the Man. I don't think he is leader of our pack. I am not even sure he wants to be. He certainly does not control the food and seems very happy to move out of the way when somebody wants to walk past. He also lets other people go out the door first—all signs that he has given up the battle for supremacy. I think he wants to be a friend rather than leader. That is good. It means he talks to me a lot. But it will cause trouble if, one day, he changes his mind and wants to be leader after all.

January 1, 1996—Hassop, Derbyshire

I ran away last night, or perhaps it was early this morning. I cannot be sure because it was dark and I was half asleep when I did it.

We were in a hotel—which is a big house with dozens of rooms. But we only had one. So I was supposed to sleep on the floor next to the bed with only a blanket out of the Man's car to lie on. I didn't mind sleeping on the floor, but the Man said, "We must do better next time. It will be our fault if he jumps on the bed during the night." I would have jumped on the bed whatever they had brought for me to sleep on.

After my early-evening walk, I was left on my own for hours. I slept in the middle of the bed until they came back, but when I woke up I could not remember where I was. I could, however, hear two distant voices calling me. So I sidestepped the Man, who stood in the open door, and ran out onto the landing. By then I was properly awake and I picked up the scent of the dogs whose call I had heard in the bedroom. It led me down the stairs, along the hall into the dining room (past people in paper hats) and out into the kitchen. I barely needed to look up. The sound and the smell planned my exact route.

There were torches burning in the drive outside the kitchen and I ran on between them, out into the road, past the church and round the back of a pub called the Eyre Arms. It was too dark to see the two Pyrenean mountain dogs that lived behind the fence in the garden. But I listened to them howling and howled back.

I had been there for about ten minutes when the Man arrived. "God, Buster," he said, "you might have been run over in the road." He had forgotten to bring my lead so he had to tie his handkerchief in my collar. His handkerchief is shorter than my lead, so he had to walk home bending down. "I knew you'd be with those dogs," he told me. Perhaps he is beginning to learn.

January 3, 1996—London

I have begun to settle down. I always expected to like it here, but at first, when I woke up in the middle of the night, I wondered if natural optimism had warped my judgment. But that was when I still thought the Man ought to let me sleep with him. Now I've stopped thinking about that and I only wake up in the night if somebody noisy goes past the front door and growling is necessary to drive them away.

January 4, 1996

Perhaps he has not learnt as much about dogs as I thought when he picked up the scent of the Pyrenean mountain dogs. He still does not realize that I don't go out just for exercise. I go out to sniff about and put my head in holes. Sometimes he is so anxious to get me into running-about territory that he hurries me past every garbage can and crumbling wall. "What's in a life so full of care there is no time to stand and sniff?" I ask myself.

January 5, 1996

Trouble on the way home from the park. All the big houses in Buckingham Gate have holes in their walls with scrapers inside them on which people used to clean their muddy boots. The holes are now used for hiding old candy papers, cookie wrappers, milk cartons and, best of all, leftover chicken. He got impatient when I wanted to make a detailed examination of a potato crisp packet, and jerked very hard on my lead. This is not how the people at the dogs' rescue expected him to behave.

January 10, 1996

I had a nasty turn this morning when, for a moment, I thought that things were turning ugly. No sooner had we got back from our walk than the Man went to my cupboard—which I had been led to believe contained nothing but biscuits and sawdust balls—and got out a piece of wood with wires sticking out at one end. Grabbing me by the collar he began to menace me with this strange object which he described as a brush.

"You will like it, Buster," he said, as he always does in preparation for doing something that I do not like at all. He then began to run the wire bits along my back. Naturally I struggled. But he held on and struck ineffectual blows in the direction of my tail. As always when in difficulty, She was called, and She operated the instrument whilst he held me down. To my surprise, the result was quite pleasant, not to say mildly erotic.

"Turn it over," the Man said—referring to the brush not to me. I am always called "him." A softer part then rubbed along my back whilst he talked the usual guff about my coat shining. He also did it on my stomach and managed to hit my sensitive bits only once.

Deliverance

January 13, 1996

He is no longer rational about the food I find on the pavement. As soon as we got out on the street tonight, he began to go on about chicken, which he says contains bones that will get stuck in my throat and choke me to death. The fast-food restaurants were in full swing. So the Man walked about staring at the pavement a yard in front of him. He has set himself up as a dropped-chicken patrol. I still found the chicken first. I'm lower down and he has no sense of smell. Of course, he told me to "Drop it" and began to force my mouth open. He does not realize that trying to take food from between my teeth puts me in more danger than letting me chew it slowly. I naturally react by trying to swallow it down whole. This morning he got to me before I had time to gulp, forced my jaws open and pushed his fingers down my throat as though he were trying to make me sick. When he scraped out the half-masticated meat and the fragments of shattered bone, he made a noise as if he was going to be ill, and said, "Disgusting!" You would have thought I had asked him to do it.

Then, of course, we went through the usual "Bad

dog" ritual. I remained remarkably forbearing. I am instinctively opposed to having food taken out of my mouth. But all I did was hang on to what I had found and therefore was rightfully mine. He got his knuckles bruised and his thumb squashed. If I had wanted to, I could have bitten his fingers off one by one. But I didn't. I think I am beginning to feel affectionate towards him. I must not let it come between me and garbage.

January 15, 1996

Where I live now, there are great smells. There were smells at the dogs' home, but I knew where they came from, and the dogs who made them thought it was their territory as well as mine. In the streets round here, the smells are all mysterious and each one has to be investigated to see if it was made by a potential intruder.

I take each one very seriously, sniffing from its origin on wall, mail slot or lamppost all the way to where it ends at the pavement's edge. Throughout the examination, my nose is as close to the flagstones as it is possible to be without wearing the end away. Once I have completed my investigation, I have a clear mental picture of the culprit and possible interloper. "Middle-aged bitch. Less than one foot from ground. Long-haired. Possibly dachshund. No threat." When a threat is located, I eliminate it by urinating on the spot that the intruder has defiled. As is well known, the last dog to urinate on a spot has staked his claim to domination of the territory. I am a miracle of nature, a walking DNA machine.

January 19, 1996

I fear I have discovered something distasteful about the Man. He collects excrement. Usually—my toilette completed—I am too busy expressing the joy of defecation to notice what's going on. But this morning, I kicked so hard with my back feet that I swung completely round. The Man had a plastic bag on his hand like a glove and was furtively bending down over the place where I had squatted. He was picking up what I had dropped.

He was very careful to retrieve every particle. He

tied the bag in a double knot, took it to one of those bins in which delicacies are stored—old teacakes, the edges of half-eaten sandwiches and cold chips—and dropped it in. Whilst all this was going on, I had to wait for the biscuit which is the proper reward of my incredibly regular habits.

January 21, 1996

Today, the excrement collection syndrome took a turn for the worse. During the early-morning walk, he tried to persuade an unknown lady to do the same—the pervert's typical behavior pattern. When the lady refused to accept his plastic bag, the Man turned nasty and started to shout about "getting us all a bad name." I cannot imagine why he should want that.

I have made excrement collection as hard as possible in the hope that I can stop him doing it. Yesterday lunchtime I backed up against a chicken wire fence and in the evening I sat on a rose bush. This morning, in St. James's Park, I crawled under a giant rhododendron. But even when he hit his head on a branch, he still wouldn't stop. I am worried in case there are more unpleasant habits yet to be revealed.

It is hard for me to struggle against my primitive instincts if the Man—who is supposed to civilize me—behaves like something out of the Stone Age.

January 22, 1996

Another example of double standards! Scratching is fine for people but forbidden to dogs. The Man scratches all the time. And everywhere. But if I put my paw within an inch of my ear, they both leap on me and exact a punishment which is out of all proportion to the crime.

The Man makes me sit between his feet, holds me round the chest with one arm and clamps my jaws shut with his free hand. Then, believe it or not, She squirts me in the ear. The squirt does not hurt, but it does feel very funny. And it is only the beginning of the torture. The Man then rubs my ear against my head, while She shouts, "Not too hard. Not too hard. The vet said do it gently."

When he stops rubbing, I can still feel the squirt

inside my ear. So I shake my head very hard. A lot of the squirt flies out and makes spots on the Man's trousers. That is one thing about being squirted in the ear that I like.

January 23, 1996—Liverpool

Yesterday we went on our first railway journey. The Man promised me it would be exciting. I think it was more exciting than he intended.

The first part was extremely boring. I sat under the table in the carriage of a railway train and he held on to my collar—usually with both hands. All I could see was feet. I don't bark, but I tried to growl at some of them. He held my jaws together as soon as I gave the first rumble. When we got off the train he said, "That wasn't bad for the first time. You'll get to like it." I shall never get to like having my jaws held together.

We then walked to what is called the Adelphi Hotel. He went in through a door which, instead of opening properly, swings round in a circle. We had to walk round inside it. I was quite frightened and I would have been more frightened still if the Man had not been inside the door with me. There was not much room and he stood on my tail, but I was glad he was there.

The Man said that I was very good in the elevator. The elevator is a very little room. When you get in it, it seems to float up in the air. I liked the floating feeling and sat very quietly in the corner. A stranger in the elevator said, "What a good dog." So when we got to the bedroom at the end of a very long corridor, I was very pleased with myself and jumped on the bed straight away. The Man pushed me off, but not before I had sniffed his suitcase. It was stuffed full of sawdust balls and biscuits.

Before he went out and left me all alone, the Man talked about me on the telephone. I always enjoy listening when the Man talks about me. "Buster is here," he said. "Nobody must come in or open the door." He then spoilt it all by adding, "He's perfectly friendly. I'm just afraid of him running out and getting lost. He's got a lot to learn." I would rather be unfriendly than have a lot to learn.

I always go to sleep when he is not there. So I do not know how long he had been gone before the lady came into the room. She was carrying towels. When I growled at her she looked very frightened. She opened the door of the little room in which he had put his suitcase and looked inside. Then she opened another door, went in and came out again without the towels. I was still growling, so she ran across the room and disappeared through the door into the corridor. She slammed the outside door behind her. But she left the other doors open.

The bathroom only smelt of soap. The little room—smaller even than the elevator—smelt wonderful. His suitcase was open, and I could see two days' rations of sawdust balls measured out in plastic bags. There were also two packets of custard cream cookies which the hotel had left for him to have when he made himself a cup of tea. I ate the custard creams first. They were only wrapped in paper. It tasted the same as the cookies.

The bags into which he had measured the sawdust balls were thick plastic, but I tore them open one by one. It all went to prove that he starves me. I ate two extra days' rations and six custard creams (and their wrapping paper) without any difficulty. At least, there was no difficulty at first.

Normally I sleep very peacefully. But that night in

the Adelphi Hotel I dreamt that there was a great worm in my stomach and, no matter how much worm medicine the Man gave me, the worm just grew and grew until it made me burst. I was very glad when the Man came back but I felt too heavy round the middle to jump up and greet him with my usual nip at his hand, tug at his sleeve and double-pawed punch in the groin. He was, however, very cheerful. "Buster," he said, "lying there like that, you look pregnant." When I still did not move, he walked across to me and began to scratch my stomach. The giant worm turned into a lead ball. So I did not even roll over on my back. "God Almighty," the Man said, kneeling down as he always does when he is worried about me. "You've been poisoned." Then he noticed that the door to the little room was open and that the plastic bags were split and empty.

I had never been out so late before. But, although my bowels were in turmoil, we walked and walked. The Adelphi Hotel is in a very noisy and dirty city so we walked through piles of litter. I did not want to eat any of it. Every time we stopped, the Man said, "Good boy. That's the idea. We're beginning to walk it off." Once a youth who was passing where I was crouched down asked his friend, "Did you make that noise or was it the dog?" His friend pushed him and he pushed his friend back. The Man said, "Watch it, this is a very sensitive dog, although he may not sound it." They all laughed. I do not know why.

As usual, I woke up at seven o'clock feeling as fit as one of the fleas I do not have. The Man had only pushed me off the bed once. The second time I climbed on, he let me stay there. He did not wake up for a long time. I am very worried there is nothing left for me to eat for breakfast.

January 30, 1996—London

He has read in one of his books that the best way to intimidate me is to make a growling sound and, believe it or not, he is trying to do it. The noise he produces is pathetic. He sounds like a cross between whooping cough and a leaky bagpipe. And he can't keep it up for more than about ten seconds. Then he chokes, splutters, wheezes and collapses into the nearest chair.

The book recommends "an additional disciplinary technique to supplement growling." It is equally incredible. He is supposed to ignore me when he comes home. The idea is that he walks in, I throw myself at him, and he takes absolutely no notice. If I go on throwing myself at him, he is supposed to go on not noticing until I realize that I am a dog of absolute insignificance who should not speak until he is spoken to.

Who writes these books? Nobody who has ever owned a dog, that's for sure. When I'm at my jumping best, I am absolutely irresistible. It is not just that I am too attractive to ignore. If he took no notice of me, I would tear his sleeve off. Dogs react best to affection.

February 2, 1996

The disciplinary offensive is now concentrating on jumping, which is totally unreasonable. I am a cheery chap. That is why, when I walk, my bottom moves from side to side even if my tail is not wagging. Everybody likes that and says, "Buster is a cheery chap." It is also because I am a cheery chap that I jump up at everybody who comes into the house and most people I meet in the street. But nobody seems to like that as much as they like my bottom moving from side to side when I walk down the street. The Man says, "I know he is a bit of a handful, but he wasn't part of a family for the first nine months." And She tells the Man, "It's in his own interests to teach him not to frighten people." It is in my own interests, handful or not, to be a cheery chappy. It is also in theirs. I can't be cheery and not jump. They'll learn with time.

February 15, 1996

I have retractable ears. They are not always the advantage that they may seem to animals whose ears are entirely immobile. When they are erect in their listening mode, people always say, "Look at Buster. He can understand every word we say." This is good, though it is not entirely true. Some words—particularly "Buster" and "breakfast"—I recognize at once, though my ears often go rigid at the sound of rustling paper in the mistaken belief that biscuits are about. However, when my ears lie flat in their hunting mode, people still say, "Look at Buster." But they think that I am about to pounce. This is sometimes true, but not always. Sometimes my ears just go flat for no particular reason.

Deliverance

February 19, 1996

The Man has still not learnt the problems I am caused by inconsistent behavior. Normally—despite my passion for cheese—all I ever get are the crumbs which bounce off his stomach and land on the floor beneath the table. Even then he makes a lot of fuss about me not picking up the bigger bits.

This morning, however, I was sent for and given a substantial piece of Stilton cheese. Admittedly the Man had rolled it into a ball. But I have absolutely nothing against the taste of human sweat and I gobbled it down with my usual enthusiasm. For the next two hours the Man followed me round the house. I had only to get up from the sofa or go into the kitchen for a bit of water for him to ask me, "Do you want to go out, Buster?" I always want to go out. But I have got used to the routine of four walks a day. To be asked the question every ten minutes from ten o'clock until twelve was strangely unnerving.

Strangely enough, instead of feeling the urge to walk at two, I was anxious for a trip to Vincent Square more than an hour earlier than usual. The Man is not normally home at lunchtime. But on what I think of as

Cheese Day, he had hung around the house all day and, to my astonishment, had my lead on within thirty seconds. We almost ran out of the door. Nothing particularly unusual happened whilst we were out. But when we got back, the Man was positively triumphant. "The worm pill works exactly as it promises on the packet," he said.

February 20, 1996—Sheffield

We have come to see the Man's mother. She is very old—probably fourteen or fifteen. She thinks she knows all about dogs and goes on about Mick, Joey, Bess, Dinah and Magnus. All of them were intelligent, loyal, well behaved, etc., etc. But none of them compares with Sally.

Sally is the ugliest bitch you've ever seen. She looks as if she is two half-dogs stitched together in the middle. Sally came from the RSPCA and was tortured when a puppy. The Man's mother kept describing the terrible things that happened to her. The stories made my tail go all limp and hang between my back legs. She then asked who had tortured me before I went to the dogs' home. She thinks all rescue dogs are tortured first.

I was not allowed into his mother's house until he had been inside and hidden all Sally's food. Although the Man's mother is a vegetarian, she says it would be wrong to force her prejudices on a dog, so she buys chicken to give to Sally. I think his mother is right, but he thinks her behavior is very funny. He believes in forcing his prejudices on people—particularly me. He shouts, "Wait! . . . Quiet! . . . Sit down!" all the time.

His mother sat in a big armchair with two cushions behind her, and Sally on the cushions. If Sally interrupted her by whining, his mother elbowed her off the cushion before continuing her stories about other people's cruelty to dogs. From the front it looked like Long John Silver and his parrot, not the Man's mother and the ugliest bitch you've ever seen. I sat next to the little table with the tea tray on it and looked winning by putting my head on one side. It did the trick at once. "Can I give him a piece of cake?" his mother asked. "No," he said. "Buster doesn't eat cake and he doesn't eat at the table."

"It's not at the table," his mother said. "And cake is good for him." Then they began to argue about what is good for me. I was terribly embarrassed. But Sally—no doubt used to that sort of thing—seemed not to mind. "I had dogs before you were born," the Man's mother said. "And killed them with rich food," he replied. He was making an unkind reference to Magnus—a Yorkshire terrier with a pedigree and long name—who died young of a heart attack. The Man says it was the cake that killed him. I put it down to the inbreeding.

February 28, 1996—Derbyshire

We have come to inspect a house which he is having mended. There are workmen everywhere and the Man says they are not even trying to get the job done on time. I am sure he is right. As soon as I try to help, they stop working—especially if they are bending down.

Outside the house there are fields and in the fields there are animals I have never seen before, called sheep and cows. Although the cows are bigger than the sheep, they are just as stupid. When I walk towards them, they run away. If they just stood there, I'd have a sniff and wander on. But when they turn their backs and run, the wolf in me takes over and I think that I am chasing my dinner through the primeval forest. The Man said, "This is going to be a problem." But I think it will be more of a problem for the cows and sheep than for me.

The house which is being mended has a lot of stairs and two gardens with steps in them. Wherever the Man may be, I can nearly always be higher than he is—that stops him thinking he is leader of the pack. At one end of the garden there is a big hedge. A Labrador puppy lives in a kennel in the garden on the other side. I tried to rescue it as soon as I was let out of the back door, but got stuck between the hedge and the chicken wire, which nobody told me was there. Whilst I waited for the Man to let me out, I howled a lot. He said that if I went on causing trouble I'd have to live in a kennel in the garden. I don't believe him.

I enjoyed the drive home. Driving—as long as you know where you are going—is great fun, especially the bit when you wake up, stand on the backseat, put your paws on the driver's shoulder and lick his ear. I think I liked the standing-up part more than the Man did.

PART II

Troubled Times

In which Buster is ill, and, after his miraculous recovery, has two unfortunate meetings, the first with a royal goose and the second with a London policeman.

March 1, 1996—London

We have been to Paws U Like, the pet shop or (as it now calls itself) the Westminster Animal Companions' Centre.

It was full of things to eat—tins of meat (all "as advertised on television" and some of them "the food of champions"), sacks full of sawdust balls I am given every morning, biscuits in dozens of different shapes and with hundreds of different tastes, white mice, gerbils, budgerigars and hamsters. We bought nothing of any value. All we brought home was a cardboard box on which was printed (in big red letters) PRECIOUS

CARGO. Underneath it said, "When you travel, make sure your pet is as safe as you are."

Inside the box there was what the Man called "Buster's braces"—scarlet webbing and buckles which he says I must wear every time I go in the car. He tried to put it on me as soon as we got home. I did all I could to help by rolling about on the floor and chewing the loose ends of the webbing, but he still could not work out which loops my legs went into and how to fasten the buckle at the back of my neck. He almost strangled me twice. Getting the harness on will add twenty minutes to every journey. With any luck he will get bored and throw it away in a week or two.

While I was choking to death, with the webbing pressing against my windpipe, the Man told me that it was all being done for my own good. He said that, being just a dog, I wouldn't see a crash coming so, when it happened, I wouldn't have braced myself and I would fly about inside the car like a giant, furry squash ball. What I can't understand is why, if he can see the crash coming, we have the crash.

Once Precious Cargo is buckled on, it is comfortable enough—and rather dashing in its way. I look as if I am about to parachute into enemy territory for purposes too secret to describe. But when it is used to make me as safe as he is, the result is a disaster. For the buckle between my shoulder blades is attached to the backseat safety belt and, although I can sit or lie down, prancing about is impossible. I am beginning to learn about caution and restraint. But without the freedom to prance, driving will lose its joy.

March 4, 1996

I have been very ill. At first I thought it was the usual stomach trouble caused by eating filth. So I rushed about looking for grass to eat. Grass makes me sick. There is no grass in our house. So I got very agitated and started chewing the doormat in the hope it would have the same effect.

It was very late, but the Man took me out and I ate a lot of real grass and was sick. I am very good at being sick. Once my stomach is full of grass I can vomit at will, contracting muscles so that I ripple from tail to head. It always makes me feel better. Last night I felt better for only a couple of hours, then I felt even worse than before. I started rushing around again—forgetting that there is no grass in the house—and bumped into all the chairs and tables. The Man got out of bed looking very frightened, and asked me, "Are you all right?" It was a silly question.

The Man knelt down and started to rub behind my ears. That is what he always does when he is worried about me. Rubbing behind my ears was the last thing I wanted, so I ran off looking for grass in the dining room. While I was under the table he made a telephone call. Then he put his trousers on over his pyjamas and we went into the car. There was no grass in the car. I did not look forward to the journey, but the Man said, "We are going to see the vet," as if I would be pleased by the news. I do not like vets. When I was very young, a vet stuck a needle in me.

The Man lifted me onto a table and the vet squeezed my stomach. I do not like strangers squeezing my stomach, so I tried to bite him. The vet said he would have to take a photograph of my insides before he could make me feel better. He then stuck a needle in me. It made me go to sleep.

When I woke up, I was in a cage in the vet's cellar. At first I was very frightened because I thought I was back at the dogs' home. So I howled a lot. Then the

Troubled Times

Man came in, knelt down and rubbed behind my ears as usual. When I saw him, I knew everything would be all right.

On the way home, he told me what was wrong with me. A bit of chicken I had picked up on the road had been wrapped in something called "plastic wrap" which is invisible. Even the photographs of inside my stomach missed it at first, so I am not to be blamed for not seeing it. The plastic wrap had blocked up my bowels. "You've got to get rid of it," he said, "or we'll have to cut you open." I think he thought that would encourage me to take the medicine the vet had given us.

The Man went on and on about not eating rubbish. "How many times have I told you that it would make you ill?" He did not expect an answer, but said, "There should be a law against dropping chicken in the street." He is wrong. Chicken that has been walked on is one of life's great delights. When he told me that taking me out at night was "like going for a walk with a vacuum cleaner," I pretended to be sick again.

March 10, 1996

Getting rid of the plastic wrap was wonderful. Every three hours for a full day he gave me a spoonful of medicine called liquid paraffin. Then we went for a walk. The walks got very boring, but the liquid paraffin had a sticky, sweet taste. After the third dose, I tried to eat the spoon.

At four o'clock this morning—I think it was the seventh walk, but I lost count—he poked about with an old walking stick he had suddenly started to carry and said, "Thank God. At last." When we got back home, I sat down and waited for a spoonful of medicine. "Look," the Man said, "Buster's addicted to liquid paraffin." Then he went to bed.

March 12, 1996

When the telephone rang this morning, I barked. It made everybody jump, including me, for I had never barked before. Now that I have started, I don't think I will ever stop. People always jump when I bark, and making people jump is one of my greatest pleasures.

Troubled Times

March 14, 1996

He has got it into his head that I am overprivileged. "Never done a day's work in your life." He does not understand that my job is looking after him. I wake him up as soon as the newspapers are delivered. I chew the mail before he opens it. I protect him from cats and keep him fit by taking him for a walk four times a day. Now that I can bark, he is protected from people who want to talk to him in the street. I make so much noise that he always says, "Sorry about this," and walks away.

The best part of my job is making him grin like an idiot by rolling on my back, lying with my legs in the air, jumping on his knee or just acting with endearing charm—which I do most of the time. Sometimes I think I have an even more important job. That is to take the blame for things I did not do. Marks on the carpet. Chairs overturned. Newspapers torn in half. Deliveries that are never made. Someone always says, "It must be Buster's fault." That part of my job is full-time.

Buster's Diaries

March 17, 1996

We went back to the vet's to make sure I am fit and well. He did not squeeze my stomach. That may be because I look so healthy or because I tried to bite him the last time he did it. The Man asked him about my food, and the vet said he had once eaten sawdust balls himself, just as a test. It was the only dog food he would consider eating. The difference between the vet and me is that he ate them once, I eat them all the time.

The vet went on to the Man about how sawdust balls kept me regular and healthy. But the Man asked, "Wouldn't he prefer boiled offal and chicken from the supermarket, like the food my mother gives to her dog, Sally?" The vet replied, "He would prefer decomposed rats that he dug up from under hedges." The vet was right. Then he said, "But it would not be good for him." That spoilt everything.

The Man said, "Perhaps we don't give him enough to eat. We always stick to what it says on the packet. But he still picks up all the filth on the road. Perhaps he is really hungry." The vet then said a very wicked thing. "Greedy dogs like Buster want to eat all the time and will eat anything."

Troubled Times

From now on, the Man will make jokes about "greedy dogs like Buster." I do not think they are very funny.

March 20, 1996

One of the nicest times is when the Man comes home at night. He always wants to sit on the sofa and watch television. I sit next to him and spill his tea by leaning against his arm just as he begins to drink it. He puts his arm round me and says, "Careful, Buster." I am never careful. I lick his face and then leap on him. She says, "He is trying to dominate you. It's not affection, it's an attempt to dominate." By then I have got my feet on his shoulders and his face is wet all over. The Man says, "It's not an attempt. He's succeeding." When I calm down, he talks to me about what he has been doing all day. Sometimes I don't understand the details, but I like the noise he makes.

The Man scratches my stomach and I lie across his knee in ridiculous positions, often with my head hanging over the side of the sofa and all four feet up in the air. I stay there until the Man says, "Let's go to bed, Buster." Then I run into my bed and go to sleep straight away. There is general agreement that I am very good at going to bed when told. That is because I would have liked to go to bed much earlier. I get bored with the Man talking to me about his day. On most nights I want to go to bed half an hour before he tells me to, but I don't like to hurt his feelings.

March 23, 1996

The Man says we have to talk seriously about discipline. He says I have no idea what the word means. That is true. I know he read about it in a book when he first adopted me. As far as I can remember, it involves constant pointless indignities.

I am no longer allowed to go through doors before he does. I have only to get my nose over the threshold for him to shout, "Back up! Back up!" I am then expected to walk backwards and stand absolutely still until he goes out in front of me. He has decided to prove that he is senior to me in the pack. It is obvious to me that he isn't. If he were leader, instead of all this

"Back up!" and "Sit!" nonsense, he would just bite me when I annoy him.

April 6, 1996

There has been an incident. The newspapers said it took place in the park, but my behavior in the park was perfectly normal. The extraordinary event happened in the street when we were on our way home from the morning's walk. A police car pulled up alongside us. Two police officers got out, one of each sort. The policeman spoke. "Excuse me, sir. Has your dog killed a goose in St. James's Park?" he asked. "Not that I know of," the Man replied, looking startled.

The policewoman patted me on the side of the head in the way that the RSPCA recommend for greeting strange dogs. She held up her hand as if she were stopping traffic. It had blood on it. "Good God," the Man said. Then the policewoman ran her finger round the inside of my collar. A lot of feathers came out. The police officer told the Man, "Get in the car." The Man got in the front seat. I jumped on his knee and, since I was facing him, I licked his face. He said, "For God's sake, not now, Buster." The policeman said, "You are not obliged to say anything, but if you fail to mention something that you subsequently use in evidence . . ." When we got home, the Man said, "You've really done it this time, Buster."

The police say I broke the law by being off the lead in the park. It is not true. I had not been off the lead. But the Man had. He was bending down doing his usual peculiar business with the plastic bag, when I gave the expanding lead a big tug. He let go. So I trotted off, and ended up in the rhododendron bushes, with the lead trailing behind me. For several minutes, he was totally out of my control and in breach of the park's regulations.

I was not alone in the rhododendron bushes for long. Suddenly a goose appeared. Geese are supposed to be frightened by dogs and fly away. But this one barely seemed to notice that I was there. It just fluttered its wings a bit and went on pecking the ground. Naturally I was offended. So I gave it a nip in the back of the neck. It waddled off, and I went into my stalking mode. When it flopped over the fence between the path and the pond, I lost interest. How was I to know that it belonged to the Queen?

Troubled Times

April 9, 1996

The newspapers found out about the goose. The Man thinks a gardener was given a biscuit for telling them. This morning there were photographers waiting for us when we went for our walk. We sat on a park bench whilst they took our picture. I was the star, gazing up at him like Man's Best Friend and licking his face. The *Evening Standard* had a billboard, "Park Murder Suspect: First Pictures."

Most of the reports were lies. Some said I had bitten the goose's head off. Others said it lay eviscerated on the path. The Man explained that the newspapers had to invent better stories than the truth—a little nip isn't news, but horrible mutilation is. And I'm supposed to be the one with the wolf inside me!

I have become very famous. This morning people stopped us in the street and told him not to thrash me or have me shot. Dog owners sent bones through the mail. There were cartoons in the *Guardian* and the *Daily Telegraph*. A dachshund called Lottie telephoned to propose marriage. He wrote back to say I was too young. People we did not know made jokes. The Man got bored with the jokes very quickly—particularly

"Has he killed a goose today?" and "Still catching your supper, is he?" I loved them. We met the police officer in the street and he said he was sure we would hear no more about the dead goose. He was wrong.

April 12, 1996

I am getting letters from all over the country. Some are from humans pretending to be dogs and some are from humans admitting to be humans. The letters which are signed by dogs all say that I was right and the goose was wrong. The letters which are signed by humans all tell the Man that he must be kind to me and not have me shot.

The Man is going to reply to everyone. He has written one letter for the dogs and another for the humans and has spent all afternoon trying to decide who should get which letter. As soon as he had mailed the first batch, he realized he had made a terrible mistake. Lulu is a House of Commons secretary not a Pekinese. I think Countess Beatrice de Villiers of Compton Basset is probably a pedigree German shepherd dog and not an English aristocrat.

Troubled Times

A solicitor has written to us about the Dangerous Dogs Act. The letter says that one day a policeman will come round and say, "Buster is a pit bull terrier type." He will then take me away and shoot me. The solicitor sent a picture of a pit bull terrier which looks nothing like me, but the Man keeps holding it up and making me stand still so that he can write down all the differences to tell the policeman when he comes round with his gun.

He has also measured me, because pit bull terriers are twenty inches from the ground to their shoulder. I am only nineteen. He keeps asking if I am likely to grow. I hope this does not mean he will try to stunt my growth by cutting down on biscuits.

He says, "If the worst comes to the worst, we will go and live in Ireland to escape from the police." He has promised we will go by boat so that I do not have to be in a box with the luggage. When he talks about going to Ireland, She always says, "Don't be stupid." What I can't work out is why it is wrong to kill a goose, but all right to shoot a dog.

Buster's Diaries

Whatever happens later in the day, we are now inseparable during the morning walk. I am never let off the lead. We walk to the park connected by the short lead. The short lead is attached to me by a noose in which I strangle myself by trying to walk faster than he is able to go. The Man says, "Walk properly," and tells people that I will soon learn. I doubt it.

Notices have been nailed to St. James's Park railings. They say, "To protect the wildlife, dogs must be on leads." The Man is very angry. He says they were nailed there after the goose attacked me. When he told me about them, I knew at once that they were a waste of public money. Dogs cannot read. Nor can they fasten themselves to leads. Or let themselves off. I am now on the long lead for all the time we spend in St. James's Park. It is not as bad as you might think.

As soon as we get into the park, the Man puts on the long lead, clipping it to my collar and—just to make sure that I don't escape—also fastening it round my neck. This takes a long time because he is very clumsy and has a lot of things to hold in his hands, including the short lead on which we came to the park.

Getting the short lead off is very difficult because he usually puts the long lead on top, rather than underneath. When the long lead is on and the short lead off, the fun really begins.

The long lead expands. I can run twenty yards before it starts to tug at my windpipe. When I run back towards him, the string disappears into a little box which is attached to the handle.

I run off as quickly as I can, accelerating with every step. Suddenly the expanding lead will expand no more. The immediate choking sensation is really rather exciting, but I have usually recovered from the blackout in time to hear the Man shout from twenty feet behind me. He knows how the expanding lead works. He bought it. But he is never ready for the moment when it is played out to its full length. As a result, his shoulder is almost pulled out of its socket.

I would still rather run about without a lead at all. That goose has a lot to answer for. Because I am bound to him, he is bound to me and we are both prisoners. I doubt if the goose would have understood. It did not look much of a philosopher.

April 24, 1996

Another totally boring day. The Man says he has a book to finish, and therefore there is no wrestling on the sofa, no chasing the rubber bone down the hall, and certainly no leaping on his knee. The Man sits at what he calls a desk—a big wooden cube with a hole in one side into which he puts his feet and legs. He likes me to sit inside the hole with my chin on his feet. This enables him to tell people how affectionate I am. Unfortunately I can only remain affectionate for about twenty minutes at a time. Then I try to jump on his knee. But because I am in the hole inside the wooden cube, I always hit my head on the wood. If he was affectionate towards me, he would say, "Poor old Buster," and give me a biscuit. But he always says, "Don't be a nuisance, Buster. I am trying to work."

May 4, 1996

I was left alone between half past seven and nine o'clock. It is the third time this week. I did not enjoy living at the dogs' home, but at least I was never left to worry if I had been abandoned for ever. When they went out, the only light they left on was in the kitchen, and all the other doors were closed. At first I thought that I had three choices of entertainment, walking about in the dark, lying in my bed or drinking water. Then I noticed that a corner of the front hall carpet was loose.

At first, I only meant to give it a little tug. But it came loose from its tacks with a very satisfying noise. So I kept tugging until half the carpet had come away from the floor. There was another hairy sort of carpet underneath and, although it was full of dust and made me sneeze, I pulled that up as well.

Although I do not claim to be an authority on these matters, I thought what I found under the two carpets looked far nicer than either of the carpets themselves. It was not floorboard, but tiles with shiny patterns on them. I could become a really first-class interior designer.

May 11, 1996—South Derbyshire

Staying in hotels is usually great fun. When the Man takes my bed it is not as much fun as when he leaves it at home. With the bed, once I go to sleep, it is not very different from being at home. But when he does not take it, I sleep on his bedspread, folded up and put on the floor in front of the window. When I sleep on the folded bedspread I always wake up at least twice and jump on him. That is the best part, especially when he wakes up with a shout.

She always shouts and pushes me off. But the Man says, "You can't blame him. He doesn't like sleeping on the bedspread. It's my fault for forgetting his bed." I wonder how long it will take before he understands that sleeping in the bed is boring. In the morning—even though I have woken him up twice—all he worries about is the bedspread. Before they bring his tea, he always says, "Quick, Bus, let's straighten out the bedspread before they find out."

Staying in the hotel in Ashford was even greater fun than usual. The owner told the Man, "There's a feral cat as big as a sheep upstairs," and said it would kill me if it caught me. The Man asked how a cat could be feral if it lived in a hotel, and the hotel owner said it used to be feral but had been tamed. I wanted to ask how tame it was, if it wanted to kill me.

Troubled Times

I was asleep when the hotel owner came with the tea, but I quickly woke up. Because he walked in without knocking, there was no chance to tie me up. To me one cat is very like another—feral or not. So off I went up the stairs. "My God!" the hotel owner said. "The cat's up there."

The hotel owner just stood there, but the Man ran up the stairs after me. He does not run up stairs very fast. Before he got halfway up, I was back on the top step with the famous feral cat in my mouth. It was not as big as a sheep. The Man began to hit me with the lead. He also shouted, "Drop it." I did not drop it. He tried to prize my mouth open like he does when I pick up old bits of Kentucky Fried Chicken. I did not open my mouth. He then started to strangle me by twisting my collar. When I could not breathe I opened my mouth. Unfortunately the feral cat fell out. The man who owns the hotel picked it up, wrapped it in a towel and took it to the vet. Afterwards the Man told me, "I don't mind the vet's bill. I'm just sorry for the cat. You wouldn't understand that." He was right.

Buster's Diaries

We have been to a new park. It is called Green Park. It is not as pretty as St. James's Park and not looked after so carefully. And it is not so much fun. There are no geese or ducks. Steve went with us. Steve comes from the Blue Cross and gives me private tuition. He knows how to look after dogs. All Steve's ideas about catching dogs are very sensible.

Steve said that when the Man catches me, he must never be angry. It is no good hitting me because he will never hit me hard enough for it to hurt. I shall always think he is playing a game. The Man looked guilty and said, "I've never even thought of hitting him." I am sure he has thought about it, though he has never done it. I cringed as though I am regularly beaten and let my tail droop between my legs—just to make him look more guilty.

Steve says I have no memory for events or incidents and that if I run away he must not shout at me when I come back. If he does, I shall think he is shouting because I have come back, not because I ran away. "The best thing to do," Steve said, "is to give him a biscuit." I like Steve.

Troubled Times

I now have a lot of friends. We meet every morning in the park. One of them is called Sandy—a real mongrel, not a first cross like I am. He carries a rubber ring in his mouth wherever he goes and will not drop it even to eat a biscuit, until he gets into a special part of the park. Then his owner throws it in the air for him, and he jumps as high as he can and catches it. There is also Henry, who is a cocker spaniel. The Man says, "You can tell he is a gentleman by his name." Henry has a piece of rope dangling from his collar so he can be caught when he runs away. That is a funny way to treat a gentleman. Lenny and Cliquot are little white Highland terriers. When the Man calls them Scotties, the ladies who own them always correct him. I cannot tell which is which. But I can always identify the lady who comes to the park with Lenny. She has a bag full of biscuits. Lenny won't eat them, so she gives them to me.

The Man tells her to stop and says he is ashamed of the way I sit down and wait to be fed. "You'd think we don't feed him," he says to the other people in the park. Then he shouts to me, "Run! You've come here to run, not to sit down." At other times he wants me to stop running and sit down. It is not surprising that I do not always do as I am told.

When we got to the park this morning, there was a new dog there called Silky. She was beautiful, and we ran about together away from all the other dogs. She is called Silky because she has silky hair, and we took it in turns to roll on our backs while the other one pretended to bite. I think I am in love for the first time. Silky's owner does not carry biscuits in his pockets. If he did, I think Silky and I might develop a permanent relationship.

June 8, 1996

Today there was a real incident in the park. It was not my fault. The Man wasn't to blame, either. However, he was not concentrating on me as carefully as he should. He kept talking to me about the soccer game that he was going to watch that afternoon—England against Holland. The price of Buster is eternal vigilance.

Even though we were in Green Park, he did not let

me off the lead because there were horses trotting about on the paths. I think they should be prohibited like bicycles. Perhaps they have been, but, because bicycles take no notice, horses take no notice either.

The Man said that it was the Queen's Official Birthday and that dozens of horses would soon gallop past the park. So we had to hurry home before they came. At one side of the park three Labradors were sniffing about on a piece of grass which was roped off. Naturally I wanted to run towards them, jump up and knock them over and roll about. He has learnt nothing from the morning when I defended myself against the goose. He dropped the lead again when he was getting the plastic bag out of his pocket. So off I ran.

When I was about a foot away from one of the Labradors, the person on the end of its lead kicked me. It did not hurt, so I had another sniff. He kicked me again and I fell over. By then the Man had caught me up. He asked, "Are you a police officer?" and started to shout, "You kicked my dog." The police officer admitted both accusations and said, "It costs six thousand pounds to train these sniffer dogs." The Man shouted, "Give me your number."

By then I was back on the lead and I was ready to

go home. But he knelt down in the wet grass and felt me all over to see if anything was broken. "This dog was out of control," the policeman told him. "I've read about him. He's been in trouble before." "Give me your number," the Man said, forgetting that the policeman had given it to him already. Another man came up to us. He was wearing a uniform and said that he was an Inspector of the park police. I thought he sounded worried about what had happened to me. He felt me all over too, and said nothing was broken. Then we went home. The Man shouted over his shoulder to the policeman who kicked me, "I shall make an official complaint." I could tell by his voice that he didn't mean it. I sometimes think domestication is overrated. I get regular meals and a warm bed, but when I get kicked there is no pack to defend me. I can't imagine the Man tearing anybody's throat out.

PART III

Improvement

In which Buster, by means of which he is unaware, is
helped by his friends to achieve greater—though not
complete—composure, and in a reflective mood,
considers his future as a human's companion,
rather than as a wolf.

June 11, 1996—London

He has been to the pet shop again. At first I used to be pleased when he came home with a sack of sawdust balls and a box of biscuits. Now I dread it, for he always brings back with him some patent idea for promoting canine happiness. Whilst he congratulates himself on being a caring person, I become a victim of the latest scheme for taking money from gullible dog owners. If I went to the pet shop with him, I might be able to show my disapproval, but I have not been allowed to go since I tried to eat the parrot.

The latest example of his gullibility is called a "halti." It is a series of straps which are fastened round my head and face and—in theory—prevent me from growling and biting. He gets very upset when people call it a muzzle. Haltis are politically correct. I can wear one and still open my mouth wide enough to eat, drink, breathe and growl and bite. But it restrains my more violent instincts.

The halti was invented by an animal psychologist who decided that a bit of webbing under the chin would make dogs cautious about how they behaved. The idea that it was cruel to undermine our self-confidence never struck him. One day, when I am with three people in the car, he will make me wear both the halti and the Precious Cargo traveling harness. I will look like a bondage freak. I admit the halti stops me from making a nuisance of myself. It is not, however, because it makes me feel vulnerable. A masculine dog does not want to draw attention to himself when he is wearing something that looks like an Alice band.

June 14, 1996

One morning I shall go mad. I don't know how I have stood it for more than six months. I accept that it is a dog's duty to wait. But the interval between returning from my walk and getting my breakfast is intolerable. I am reconciled to everyone finishing their breakfast before mine is even thought of. But now the process of transferring food from bucket into bowl is artificially extended. Not only is it carefully measured out, but the bowl is methodically washed every morning. When did a dog ever catch food poisoning because its bowl had been left unwashed for a week? They only do it to annoy because they know it teases.

June 21, 1996

I thought that human companionship would be enough, but since I met Silky I have begun to feel a desperate need of female canine company. Unfortunately, there is none at home. Brief and occasional meetings in the park do not provide an opportunity for the sort of relationship which I have begun to crave. As a result I am, from time to time, driven by mysterious forces into what I know to be bizarre behavior. But I am unable to resist.

I find myself sitting in my basket and howling like a wolf baying at the moon. I expect the Man to react violently, for he has no ear for the true music of the wild. But his complaint makes no sense. Instead of objecting to what he hears, he raves on about something that I can't even see.

"For God's sake, Buster!" he cries. "It's happening again. Worse than ever. We're going to walk it off." I am then dragged down the road at what he calls "light infantry pace." Strangely enough, at first I do not want to stop at the usual lampposts and garbage cans. Happily, after a while, the old urge to make my mark returns. "Thank God for that," the Man says, and we immediately go back home, where he begins to talk seriously about me.

Tonight the Man said he "didn't know whether to be envious or embarrassed." She always tells him not to be foolish and face up to the real problem. So he began to argue with a vet who was not there. "Whatever he says, I hate the idea. We're supposed to look after him and he suggests we mutilate the poor little chap." The Man then got angry. "I've told you. It's nothing to do with my own complexes. I haven't got any. I just don't want to hurt him." Before he went to bed, he was near to tears. "OK. So he'll be happier. It's supposed to be for his own good. Perhaps we should protect him from running under a bus by cutting off his legs as well." I did not like all the talk about cutting my legs off, so I jumped into my bed and howled. "Oh God!" said the Man. "It's happening again. That's twice in twenty-five minutes." Even though it was time for bed, he telephoned the vet and talked about me very seriously indeed.

"Are you sure it will be better for him? . . . If you're sure he won't feel any pain, or change character. . . . It's not being fierce that is a problem, it's being frustrated. . . . Probably in Derbyshire. . . . My mother's vet in Sheffield. . . . He'll have a garden in case walking is difficult. . . . Nevertheless, we'll have it done up there."

June 22, 1996—Derbyshire

We drove up to Derbyshire late last night. This morning we went on our walk very early. He kept patting me as if we were saying goodbye. I like to run about smelling the bushes where the sheep have been and pushing my head into rabbit holes, but he kept calling me back and patting me. But he did not give me one biscuit. And when we got home, he did not give me any breakfast. Instead he listened to a message from his mother's vet. It said, "Get here by ten o'clock."

I am always depressed on the way to see a vet. For, whatever else they do, vets always end up sticking needles in me. But this morning I felt particularly gloomy. The Man was so sad that I thought that he was going to cry. And I always share his emotions.

There was a guinea pig in a cage in the waiting room, but we went straight into the surgery. The Man lifted me onto a table and a young lady with long red hair listened to my heartbeat down a stethoscope. The Man turned me round and held my head under his arm. A funny feeling where I sit down made me wriggle a bit, but I did not try to bite him. I never try to bite the Man. He said, "It will be all right, Buster. It's just a way of taking your temperature." The young lady with red hair must have realized that the Man was worried about something, for she said, "There's really nothing to worry about. He won't even notice, and if his character changes, it will be for the better."

Improvement

I am not sure what she was talking about. It could not have been me. My character is beyond improvement.

"Can I have some painkillers?" the Man asked. "They won't be necessary," the young lady with long red hair said. "I'd like them all the same," the Man told her. Then he asked, "Is there an emergency night telephone number?" and was told that wouldn't be necessary either. But the Man repeated what he had said: "I'd like it all the same." Then he added something very interesting. "I also want a Buster collar."

I have several collars already. One is specially for fleas. None of them is a Buster collar, which (when the young lady got it out of the cupboard) I thought was a lampshade. "He won't scratch," she told him, "because he won't know what's happened." The young lady then stuck a needle in me. That is when I realized that, although a woman, she was a vet.

I fell asleep. When I woke up I felt very frightened. But I had only whined for about five minutes when the young lady vet came in with my collar and lead. I barked when she tried to put it on, but not enough to stop her. The Man was waiting outside. He knelt down as soon as he saw me and rubbed behind my ears. When I licked his face, there was a salty taste as if he was crying. I did not make a fuss about it, because I did not want to embarrass him.

"You see," the young lady vet with long red hair said, "he's as right as rain. Doesn't know it's happened. Perhaps a bit woozy for an hour or so. . . ." The Man led me ever so slowly towards the door. I misjudged where it was and walked into the wall. It didn't hurt.

July 3, 1996—Sheffield

This afternoon's visit to his mother produced the best argument yet. They argue every time we go there. But today they argued without ever telling each other what they were arguing about. It all started as soon as the Man had hidden Sally's food. We walked together into the room where his mother was sitting and, the moment he sat down, he patted his knee so that I would jump into his lap. "There you are," he said. "You see. . . ."

The Man's mother looked as if he had just bitten her. "Don't tell me you have . . ." she cried, tears fill-ing her eyes. "You haven't! You wouldn't! No son of mine would!" The Man said, "It was for the best.

Three vets said so. It was for his sake." The Man sounded very nervous.

"Rubbish," his mother shouted. "You're just joking, aren't you? You haven't really . . . ?" Then she gave a smile which she meant him to know was not genuine. He said quickly, "I have, Mother. It's all over and we can't put them back, can we?" It was his turn to give a false grin. His mother told him, "Don't be horrible." I could not help him by joining in the fun, since I had no idea what was going on. "Does he look any different?" the Man asked. I assumed that he was trying to change the subject by talking about me. "He never even knew it had happened."

I was trying my best to work out what it was that I did not even know had happened, when the Man's mother got a box of chocolates from the cupboard next to her chair and began to feed them to me one by one. "Poor little chap," she said. The Man groaned. "For God's sake, Mum." For a moment, he forgot all about the prohibition on blasphemy which always comes into force when we go to see his mother. He rolled me over as if he was going to tickle my stomach and said, "I tell you he's no idea. If you don't believe me . . ."

The Man's mother put her hands over her eyes.

"You know," she said, "I can't stand even the thought of cruelty." She went on to describe Sally's suffering before she was rescued. I'd heard the description a dozen times so I rolled back onto my side and went to sleep. When I woke up she was talking about brutality to pigs.

July 16, 1996—London

The Man says he is taking the rap for me—even though I know he was to blame. He read in the paper this morning that he is to be prosecuted under the Royal Parks Act 1786 as amended 1977 in so much as he failed to keep me under control and allowed me to harm, injure or kill wildlife, to wit a greylag goose. The Crown Prosecution Service telephoned to say they were sorry that it was in the paper before he was told about it. They said the newspapers had got the details all wrong but the basic fact was correct. The Man said, "You could make up for leaking it to the newspapers by dropping the prosecution." The Crown Prosecution Service did not reply.

Improvement

July 21, 1996

When we went for our walk, a man called Charles Anson stopped us outside Buckingham Palace. He said, "There's a famous face." The Man thought that he meant him, but he meant me. Charles Anson used to work for the Man in the Foreign Office, but now he talks to newspapers for the Queen. So he had read about my prosecution. "I want you to know," he said, "that your monarch is totally on your side. If it's dog versus goose, she's for the dog." The Man asked, "Will she come to court as a character witness?" Charles Anson said that he seriously doubted it.

I blame Anson for giving him the idea of fighting the case. First we went to St. James's Park to look at the notices. The Man got very angry when he saw the little notices with big letters, by the edge of the pond, which he says were screwed to the railings after the goose and I had our disagreement. Unfortunately, the big notice with little writing (which is fastened to the gate) has been there for years. It says that I must be kept under control. So we can't plead ignorance. The Man's other idea is that the goose would have flown away if the Queen had not clipped its wings so that it would never leave Buckingham Palace. As we walked home, he talked about basing our defense on the Queen's wanton cruelty. Then he telephoned his solicitor and decided instead to plead guilty to both offenses by sending a cringing letter.

August 3, 1996

The Man asked me this morning why I am so stupid about traffic. Fortunately, he does not expect me to reply to his questions, for I did not know the answer. I ought to realize that a bus, traveling at twenty miles per hour, could squash me flat on the road. I know that if I saw a cat on the opposite pavement I would forget about the bus and get squashed. So, every time we go out, he has to stop me from walking into certain death. It is all very puzzling. I am certainly not stupid, but I act stupid on main roads. Perhaps it is because the wolf that sleeps inside me never knew about buses.

The one thing about which the Man is always really stern is sitting down on curbs before we cross—me, that is, not him. Even when other people run off to the other side of the road, he says, "Wait, Buster, for the little green man to walk." I have never seen the little green man on the traffic light. Perhaps only human beings can see him, in the way that only sheepdogs can hear high notes on whistles. Anyway, as soon as the little green man comes into his view, we walk across the road—very slowly and on a very short lead.

August 15, 1996

We all thought I had learnt months ago to come back when called. And generally speaking I have. There is, however, a special problem on summer evenings which I just don't know how to overcome. All over the park people are sitting down on the grass and eating sandwiches. The ham and the tuna, the salt beef and the chicken are all exactly at my eye level and, more important, at my nose level as well. I have now reached a degree of self-control which I think would allow me to look and sniff without snatching and eating. But the people who own the sandwiches are too stupid to understand.

You may find it hard to believe, but if you run at

full speed towards a recumbent American teenage tourist with a frankfurter hot dog in her hand, she will immediately scream and throw the hot dog in the air. Of course, I catch it (admittedly usually after the second bounce) and swallow it before the Man can snatch it from me. I then run on to the next group of holiday-makers in the hope that they will behave in the same way. They always do. Their stupid conduct would have severely jeopardized my training program, had the Man not stopped taking me to the park in the evening.

August 24, 1996

I am beginning to learn to come back when called. It is very much in my own interests. If I can be relied on to return as required, I can be let off the lead when in the park. I shall then be free to urinate against the trees of my choice. Choosing my own trees is very important, since I urinate not to relieve my bladder but to prove that I was the last dog on the spot.

Unfortunately, hard though I try, I sometimes fail to heed the call. There is no particular reason for my disobedience. I just wander off aimlessly or run nowhere in particular. The Man shouts, whistles and holds biscuits in the air in the hope that the wind will blow the smell towards me. No matter how long it takes to attract my attention, he always gives me a biscuit when I return. In a month or two, the idea of eating and doing what I am told will be connected in my mind and I shall swallow my pride and hurry back to swallow a biscuit as quickly as possible. In the meantime, there is nothing to be gained by saying I have "cloth ears." I have very handsome ears and they are not made of cloth.

September 1, 1996

Last night we went for a walk by the place where the police dogs live. I don't think they are the dogs who disarm desperadoes and rescue children from burning buildings. They are the sniffers who find where drugs are hidden and explosives planted. Sniffing is one of my greatest pleasures, but I would not like to do it for a living. If I became a police dog, I would disarm criminals and rescue children from burning buildings.

We never see the sniffer dogs. But we do hear

them moaning. I take no notice, for it is their territory not mine, but he always uses their noise as an excuse to go on about my failure to earn my living. He thinks he is being funny. I find it very hurtful.

That does not stop him going on about dogs with brandy barrels hanging from their necks who rescue climbers from the snow, dogs who guard factories, dogs who round up sheep, dogs who collect dead pheasants, dogs who pull sledges, dogs who chase foxes and dogs who lead blind people about. He says that in Israel there are dogs who go across the border into Lebanon, chasing terrorists. They have time bombs fastened to their backs. I think he invented it, just to make me feel grateful. "Your problem, Buster," he always says, "is that you don't have a trade."

September 13, 1996

I have been thinking about which job would suit me best if I were ever allowed out on my own. I think I would make a wonderful detective. I am, by nature, curious. I cannot pass a hole without wanting to put my head in it or walk alongside a wall without wanting to look over it.

Improvement

I sniff at every black bag I pass in the street and try to make the Man turn his pockets out to prove that he does not have biscuits concealed about his person. Sad, really. Fate has made me a security guard when I should have been head of the local police department. Fortunately, I am indomitably cheerful by nature.

September 19, 1996

The Man has invented a new way to stop me making a nuisance of myself at breakfast when I am supposed to sit under the table—ideally with my head affectionately on his feet. If he had his way, I would be fed as soon as we get back from our walk. But She is in charge of food and, being a stern disciplinarian, She makes me wait—just to prove who's boss.

I can contain myself in patience until their breakfast is over, contenting myself with the toast crumbs which bounce off the Man's stomach. But when I sense that even he can't eat any more, I pop up between his knees and push my nose up to table level. Sometimes I bang my head, but I don't mind. If he is leaning back and there is room, I get my paws onto his lap.

"Bad dog, Buster," he shouts, and hits me over the head with the newspaper he is reading. He has done it each morning for the last week and, although it does not hurt, I still don't expect it so it always gives me a nasty shock and I gently subside back onto the carpet. His blows are absolutely indiscriminate. If he is reading the *Guardian*, he hits me with the *Guardian*. If he has *The Times* in his hand, I get *The Times*. He calls it the up-market deterrent. This morning it was the *Daily Mirror*. He said I had been subject to the ultimate humiliation.

October 10, 1996—Derbyshire

Today the Man took even longer than usual to get ready for our walk. He was late getting up. So I was bursting from the moment that he woke me. I waited patiently enough while he put on the usual seven or eight layers of clothes. Watching him lace up his walking boots (which always takes about an hour) was more difficult to endure calmly—particularly since they are an affectation and totally unnecessary for the couple of miles we stroll across fields. I knew that, even when he had struggled into the overcoat with the belt I chewed, there would still be a long delay while he searched for the long lead, the short lead, his keys and his cell phone, all of which would be hidden in different parts of the house. Why he does not put them in the same place every night, I shall never know. Then, as usual, before we got as far as the door, he remembered that he had to go back into the kitchen and get a plastic bag and biscuits to give me when the bag was filled. I gritted my teeth and tried to think of something else.

It was raining, so, after a single step into the yard, he decided he needed a hat. Then he thought it prudent to change from the top coat with the belt I chewed into the waterproof jacket with the pocket I tore. That, he quickly decided, would expose his legs to the storm. He went back for his long trenchcoat. By the time he had fastened all the complicated buckles and belts, the rain had got much worse. So he unlaced his boots and put his Wellingtons on instead. I just sat there until I was quite sure he was ready. Then I was so happy to be on the move that I got the lead wrapped round my legs. "Buster," he said, "you are a terrible nuisance in the mornings." I put it down to his embarrassment at the unfairness of it all. I have no shoes and one suit which I wear night and day, summer and winter. He has so many clothes that it takes him an hour to get ready for our morning walk. And he says I am a nuisance! My only consolation is that my one suit looks so good on me.

October 21, 1996—London

We are facing a communications crisis. It is not my fault. He reads all those books and newspaper articles about how to look after me, but, although we have lived together for months, he still does not give me clear and consistent instructions. I am not sure how hard he tries. Whoever is to blame, I'm the one who always gets into trouble. Sometimes I think he expects me to read his mind.

I want to do what pleases him—particularly since pleasing him is usually followed by a biscuit—but I need to know what he wants. Take, for example, "jumping up"—when I assume the heraldic position of Buster Rampant (which is more or less what I am at the time) and scratch at him with my front paws. Unfortunately, he is never able to make up his mind whether or not he likes it. All I can be sure of is that he does not find it much fun when he is wearing his pyjamas. Fully dressed, he has been known to take my paws in his hands and cry, "Shall we dance? One, two, three. Look! I'm Yul Brynner and Buster is Deborah Kerr." No sooner am I vertical than he begins to rub behind my ears, scratch my stomach and (when nobody is looking) lean down so that I can lick his face. But at other times, he either sways out of my path so my front paws hit the floor with a thump, or just shouts at me. It is all very disturbing. A dog needs certainty.

November 1, 1996

Living with someone who cannot decide what is right and what is wrong is very hard, especially for a dog whose father was an Alsatian and who is, therefore, genetically inclined towards obedience. The problem was made worse today when the Man couldn't remember the right words to describe what he wanted me to do. He was totally confused about "Down."

There is absolutely no doubt what "Down" means.

When the word is spoken clearly and in an authoritative tone—particularly if the speaker is holding a biscuit—"Down" means "Imitate one of the lions at the foot of Nelson's Column by lying absolutely still, stomach flat on floor, back legs outstretched and front legs neatly side by side until you are told otherwise." It does not mean "Stop jumping up." Yet today, immediately after breakfast, when I made a speculative leap to test the sort of mood he was in, he pushed me away and said, "Down," in an absentminded sort of way. What I needed was either a rub behind the ears or a "No, Buster. Bad dog." It is a miracle that I am not totally out of control.

November 13, 1996

The dog warden—who is a lady—came round this morning. At first I was very frightened. I thought she had been sent by the police to decide whether or not I am a pit bull terrier and should be shot. In fact, she was very nice and talked about me in an affectionate way. She said she wanted us to avoid trouble. I sat very still. She gave us a leaflet.

The leaflet described the things that dogs can do

in my neighborhood. It also described what they cannot do. The "cannot do" part of the leaflet took up most of the space and even the "can do" things can be done only on the pavement, not on the road.

There was a horrible description of roundworm (*Toxocara canis*), an advertisement for something called easy-to-use pooper-scoopers, and a picture of a Fido machine. A man was leading it along on the end of a wire. Owning a Fido machine cannot be half as much fun as having a real dog. You can take it for a walk, but you can't stroke or pat it and it can't jump on your knee or lick your face. And the Fido machine cannot bark. The leaflet says that barking is important. "One of the pleasures of owning a dog is hearing its welcoming bark when you return home." Quite right.

The leaflet spoilt everything by saying that "a barking dog can cause friction between neighbors" and suggesting that dog owners go to obedience classes. I think the Man would be very boring if he was obedient all the time. If he always walked simply by my side without ever making a noise or jumping about, life would not be much fun for me. He would be just like a cocker spaniel—all floppy ears and dopey expression. I think men need to show a bit of character.

The dog warden told the Man that, for my own sake, I ought to join Pettrac National Pet Registration scheme. When he asked her what I would have to do, she told him, "Have a chip implanted under the skin at the back of his neck." The idea makes no sense to me. When we are out late at night and I find a chip in the road, I am not allowed to eat it. I cannot imagine enjoying having one buried under my fur even if, as the dog warden promised, it would mean that I could be "held on the national computer." I get held far too much anyway. But the Man is a sucker for fancy ideas. I fear that I shall soon be implanted.

Anyway, we are safe from the dog warden for a while. She is going to have a baby. After she had gone, the Man said, "At least, Buster, nobody will be able to blame you for that."

November 20, 1996

According to the newspapers, the Man was in court this morning, charged with behavior "contrary to Regulations 3(6)(b) of the Royal and other parks and gardens regulations 1977." In fact, he wasn't really in court at all.

Improvement

A solicitor went for him and read out the letter the Man had written. It took him almost a whole day to write and, in the end, he decided to tell the truth about bending down to collect my excrement and relaxing his grip on the long lead. He really has no excuse for letting me behave like that. As I have made clear more than once, the price of Buster is eternal vigilance.

After about fifty telephone calls with the solicitor, he decided that the letter should include what he calls a joke. "In fact, Buster was never off the lead. Unfortunately I was." As soon as he had mailed the letter he started to worry about the joke costing him an extra £100. The rest of the letter was very pious. "I am naturally most disturbed by the news that he killed the goose and very much regret its death."

As we might have expected, it was the *Evening Standard* which was waiting for us when we went out for our morning walk, and their photographer took more pictures of me. The Man said he was going to stand by me. The reporter followed us all the way to Green Park. I was careful to sit very still when we had to wait for the traffic lights to change. When we got to Buckingham Palace, a policeman said, "I see the reptiles have been let out today." I thought he meant me, but the Man knew better. He asked the policeman what would happen if he strangled the reporter and the policeman replied, "I would shake you by the hand." Despite this encouragement, the Man did not strangle the reporter, who went home when we got to the muddy part of Green Park.

The solicitor telephoned at lunchtime to say that the Man had been fined £25 for not keeping me on a lead and £50 for letting me kill the goose. He would also have to pay £200 costs. The Man did not seem to mind. He was much more upset to learn that "the place was full of journalists."

November 21, 1996

This morning began last night. The Man would not go to bed until today's papers were on sale near Victoria Railroad Station, and I had to stay awake and go with him. A Rastafarian offered to buy me for £50. The Man said, "Not for five thousand," and the Rastafarian said, "He is not worth five thousand." I had liked him until then.

All the papers had stories about me. The Man says I must be careful not to be spoilt by fame, and he has refused to allow me to go on television. I heard him say on the telephone, "All it needs is an exploding lightbulb or a cameraman with a sandwich and all hell will be let loose."

The newspaper stories all contain terrible puns—up in front of the beak, fowl play and goose being cooked. The Man said, "You come out of it better than I do. You're only an assassin. I'm a journalist." I don't think that I come out of it badly at all.

November 27, 1996

The Man has joined Passports for Pets. It is an organization that wants me to go on holiday to France. In fact I can already go on holiday to most places. But I am not allowed back.

All the French dogs are mad and foam at the mouth and run around France biting people. The people they bite die. The dogs they bite die as well, but not until they have bitten people and killed them. I cannot go to France because, if I did, a French dog would bite me and, when I came back, I would bite Englishmen and kill them.

Passports for Pets wants to stop all this happening, but I am not sure how they will do it. I am not even sure that I want to go to France.

December 3, 1996—Derbyshire

I think I have fallen in love again. This morning, when we went on our usual walk across the fields to the old railway line, a golden-haired retriever bounced up to me, and for a moment I forgot about the sheep that I was hoping to turn into mutton. I fear my emotions were embarrassingly obvious, for the Man said, in his most coy voice, "What about Silky? Have you forgotten her?" Of course I've forgotten her. I can't remember much for more than twenty-four hours—though, if we ever meet again, all the old feelings will come flooding back.

The golden-haired retriever is called Flora and her hair—which is more like copper than gold—shines in the sun. She lives in a family of six other dogs. All of them were out for a walk with her, but she came straight over to have a sniff at me. I sniffed back at once. The Man said, "Better come away, Buster." But

Flora's owner said, "No problem at the moment. But I'm counting off the days." I'm counting off the days too. We will be back in Derbyshire next week.

December 10, 1996

Flora is lost to me for ever. This morning, on our way to the old railway line, we saw half a dozen dogs coming towards us across the fields and the Man said, "Look, Buster. It's Flora." It wasn't. And it would have been much better if I had not been reminded about her.

The Man asked Flora's owner where she was. I do not know what the answer was but the Man said—with remarkable lack of sensitivity—"Well that's that, Buster. When you next see Flora she'll be an old married lady with puppies to look after. She's gone away to spend the week with another thoroughbred golden-haired retriever." My only consolation is that I have a memory span of only twenty-four hours.

December 23, 1996

The Man went mad this morning. I hope that it is only temporary. Usually I get into trouble if I go within a yard of his bathroom door. But just before lunchtime, he dragged me inside. I had barely begun to shake a towel to death when he picked me up and dropped me into the bath. It was half full of warm water.

Not content with it lapping against my stomach, he splashed it all over me. Then he got a bottle from a shelf and poured something sticky on my back. "Don't worry, Buster," he said. "It's specially for dogs. If it goes into your eyes, it won't hurt." Until then I had not thought about it going into my eyes, so I had not worried. I started to worry when he told me not to.

The sticky stuff out of the bottle bubbled all over me and he splashed me again until it was all washed off. That is when I knew he was mad. Why else would he put the sticky stuff on me one minute and wash it off the next?

The Man let the water out of the bath whilst I was still inside. Then he rubbed me with the towel I had tried to shake to death. That was the only nice part of the whole thing. He did not get me dry, so I shook my coat. Then we were both wet all over. The

Man retaliated by insulting me. "At least you don't smell any more," he said. Everybody knows I am very clean. It said so on the advertisement when the dogs' home put me up for sale.

December 24, 1996

Everybody is behaving very strangely. The Man has brought a tree into the house and planted it in the hall. The tree has very strange fruit and flowers. The fruit rattles when I shake the tree and the flowers glow when the Man switches the lights on. I am not allowed to go anywhere near the tree.

There is another tree—only much bigger—on the grass opposite our house. As soon as it got dark, the flowers lit up and thousands of people arrived to stand round it and make a noise. Most of them made the same noise but, with my expert dog ears, I could tell that one or two were making a different noise from the rest. I sat in the window between the curtains and the glass and barked. I did not bark very convincingly. There were too many people for one dog to frighten away.

PART IV

Tolerance

In which Buster meets—in diverse circumstances—a variety of other animals and struggles, with different degrees of success, to regard them as friends.

January 1, 1997—Derbyshire

The Man got up late this morning and said that he always regretted it afterwards. I think he meant that he regretted keeping me waiting. We did not go on our long walk until the afternoon. In the fields on the way to Baslow, there was still a lot of snow on the ground. I like snow. It tickles my stomach. The Man says it makes me more stupid than ever.

On the way home I was let off the lead when She said that I "needed to stretch my legs." The Man said, "We'll regret it," but, as usual, She got her way. I stretched my legs by running back to where the cows were—three fields away. I did not harm them, but herded them into a friendly little group by running round them in ever-decreasing circles. The Man said, "Look at Buster, he's evolved from hunting to animal husbandry," and She said, "Don't be stupid. Catch him."

Since, unlike me, the Man always does what She tells him, he tried to catch me and fell down in the snow several times. The farmer, who came up in a tractor, said, "You're just making him more excited. He's doing no harm. Just wait till he gets tired." It took a long time for me to get tired. When I did and went back to the Man, he forgot which lead he should use, and I had to walk home so close to him that he stood on my paws twice. He kept saying, "I blame you for that." I don't think he was speaking to me.

January 3, 1997

I can't honestly say I like being left alone in Derbyshire, but it is better than being left alone in London. In Derbyshire, I am left to run up and down the stairs. So I can sit on the window seat on the front landing and growl at everything that comes past. I can also push open one of the bedroom doors and lie on the bed. The Man thinks he fastens it shut before he goes out, but the latch doesn't work.

Running up and down stairs and barking is immensely tiring work, so I normally doze off after an hour or two. However, it is absolutely essential that I wake before the Man opens the front door, otherwise he suspects that I have not been properly vigilant and mocks me. He has begun to creep down the path—and sometimes even goes round to the back and comes in through the kitchen. If I am not there the moment he gets inside the house, he shouts, "Very slow, Buster. Very slow." He knows I hate being laughed at. He expects me to slink away in shame. Of course I just jump at him in the usual way.

January 11, 1997

There was an unfortunate misunderstanding on our railway journey from London this afternoon. Usually I quite enjoy the journey to Derbyshire. I lie, with my head on the Man's foot, under the table and allow the rhythm of the swaying engine gently to rock me to sleep. For most of the time, he keeps his fingers in my collar, ready to reassure me that all is well if anybody to whom I may take exception passes.

All went well as far as Leicester. He bought a large Kit Kat from the trolley service and, as usual, all I got was a bottle of water. Just north of Market Harborough, I fell asleep and dreamt, not of rabbits and rats as usual, but of a man and a dog who enjoyed an ideal relationship. The man drank the water and the dog had the large Kit Kat.

I blame the ticket collector for what happened next. At first he did a very good job—taking great care not to stand on my tail when he punched the Man's ticket. Then he got chatty with the Man. First he talked about the Labour Party, then about Sheffield Wednesday soccer club. The Man only likes talking to me during train journeys. But he said "Yes" and "No" a lot. Before the ticket collector left, he leant over and tried to shake the Man's hand. Before you judge me, put yourself in my position.

I was lying half asleep on the floor of a swaying railway carriage and my view of what was going on above was obscured by the table. All I saw was a quick movement of feet and an arm moving swiftly towards the Man. From where I lay, it was impossible to distinguish between a handshake and a blow. I only did my duty.

Fortunately, the damage was done to the trousers, not the leg and, at the time, it seemed likely that it could be easily remedied. The tear, admittedly from hip to ankle, ran down where the seam already fastened two pieces of cloth together. So it could have been worse. But the Man still offered to pay for a new pair.

The ticket collector was very good about it, rightly saying that it was my job to look after the Man. He added that he would not like to meet me in a dark alleyway. Quite right. I took that as a compliment. For the next mile or two the Man held my collar a bit too tight. But everything seemed all right until the head ticket collector came round and said, "My colleague told me of what happened. The dog attacked him." By "the dog," he meant me.

The Man, very reasonably I thought, said, "He only caught his trousers." But the head ticket collector replied, "It might have been his leg." He went on to give a lecture about what a danger I could be to passing children and elderly ladies who could not spring back.

The Man does not like lectures, but he listened politely until the head ticket collector told him he should buy a muzzle. Then he pointed to the hated halti, which was still round my head just below my eye and above my mouth. "That stops him biting," the Man said. The head ticket collector told him, "It doesn't seem to be working." The Man looked very upset. "It's a muzzle for you, Buster," he said. "Paws U Like as soon as we get back to London."

January 14, 1997—London

We have bought a patent muzzle. It is called the Baskerville and it is made of plastic. He normally says that only real leather is good enough for a dog of my quality, but he justified buying a plastic Baskerville with the pretense that he found the name funny. Apparently, it reminded him of a basket—which it looks like when you hold it up by the straps—a wicker vest and a hound that lived on Dartmoor and tore out the throats of innocent passersby. "The problem," he said, "is that when you wear it, people will think you're very fierce." I want people to think I am very fierce. I

112

am not as fierce as I was—which is why I like the Baskerville giving the wrong impression.

January 21, 1997

I would much rather wear the Baskerville than the halti. I hardly know when the Baskerville is on. I can open my mouth inside it and the Man can push tiny cat biscuits (called Kitbits) through the plastic bars. But the best thing about it is the impression it creates. The Man was right to say it would frighten people. I only wear it on railway trains. But he has to put it on before we get to the station, so I walk the full length of the platform looking as if I am too vicious to be trusted. One lady asked, in awe, if I was a rottweiler. Her question seemed to make the Man angry. He told her my name is Hannibal Lecter, which is not true. There is much to be said for a muzzle. But I wish it wasn't made of plastic. I deserve something with more class.

Buster's Diaries

This morning in the park I made an understandable but terribly embarrassing mistake. A person, standing with his feet absolutely still, was moving the rest of himself about in a strange way. First he held his arms in the air and made them sway like branches. Then he fluttered his fingers like leaves. The Man now claims that the person was doing something called "Tai Chi" to guarantee his tranquillity during the day. But, at the time of the incident, I think we were both equally confused. I, at least, admit my error. I thought the person was a tree. I am sure it is possible to be tranquil even with wet shoes.

February 7, 1997

I have begun pointless barking. I have enjoyed pointless running and pointless jumping for some time, but pointless barking is a new enthusiasm. My barking is now as undiscriminating as Lizzie Bennett's coughs. Because he was worried about the neighbors complaining, the Man looked up "barking" in his dog book. It appeared immediately after "bad breath."

Barking, the book said, is employed to intimidate, welcome or to call up reinforcements. Where I live you could wear your vocal cords down to their roots and reinforcements would not arrive. There is something that yaps next-door-but-one and a miniature Scots terrier twenty yards up the road. I doubt if either of them can hear me and if they could they are not the sort of dog which you expect to have much esprit de corps. Even if they came, they would not be much use. There were bigger rats in the garden where I was born.

February 14, 1997

This morning, in the park, I was bitten on the ear by Oscar, the mad Italian retriever. I blame the Man. He calls Oscar "Benito" and told me that as he was Italian I had nothing to be afraid of, because he would run away at the first sight of danger. That was not true, and I have a tear in my ear to prove it.

The Man took me to the vet straight away where, naturally enough, a needle was stuck in me. This time,

I did not go to sleep. The vet said the needle was a pre-caution in case Oscar's teeth were dirty and my ear turned septic and fell off, and that the tear in my ear would heal very quickly but I might have an unsightly scar unless he put a stitch in my ear. The Man—who I suspect is jealous of my good looks—said, "If it's just cosmetic, we won't bother." I shall go through life scarred.

All this has made me even more doubtful about Passports for Pets. Until this morning I thought dogs ought to be allowed to travel abroad without being locked up in kennels when they came back to England. Now I am not so sure. I think it's right that English dogs should be allowed to go abroad. But I do not think that foreign dogs—particularly Italians—should be allowed to come here. If we are not careful, we will be swamped.

February 19, 1997—Derbyshire

I have decided to limit pointless barking to the house, where the Man is amused by it whether or not he says, "Shut up, Buster. You're driving me mad." Out on walks

Tolerance

I now bark with more discrimination—as befits an increasingly sophisticated dog.

When we pass dogs on the road, in fields or when I am pulling the Man up one of the nearby hills, I never bark first. If I can get near enough, I jump at them, but it is always a silent jump. But if they start to bark, I always bark more loudly and for much longer. That shows who is boss.

I still bark when he stops to talk to people. But not for long. He has now learnt to scratch my head whilst in conversation. Although I am impatient to move on, the head-scratching always keeps me quiet.

Back in London we often walk past the home of a big, fawn-colored boxer called Jake. He always barks at us in a very loud voice and runs along the inside of his garden fence so that he can keep barking at close quarters. I never reply. He is guarding his territory just as I guard mine, and must be respected for the thorough way in which he does the job.

My reason for not replying to Jake is quite different from the reasons for which I ignore the little yelping Scottie in Station Road up here in Derbyshire. The little Scottie lives with a cat so, no matter how much he yelps, I do not condescend to notice him.

Buster's Diaries

We were joined in the park this morning by two retrievers we had not seen before. Their names are Ben and Novak. Their owner, who was very grim and serious, is called Norman or Lord Tebbit. The two dogs are better trained than any other dogs in the park. They may be better trained than any other dogs in the world. Norman or Lord Tebbit makes them sit side by side on the path. Then he throws a ball and tells Ben to fetch it. Novak sits absolutely still until Ben returns. Then it is Novak's turn to get the ball and Ben's turn to sit still. None of the other dogs—the regulars who run about together each morning—dared go anywhere near them. Like our owners, we just watched in terror and amazement.

When Norman or Lord Tebbit had taken Ben and Novak home, some of the humans said that they were glad that their dogs did not behave like that. I did not believe them. I think they were envious. Although I would hate to be so well behaved, I liked Norman or Lord Tebbit. I thought he was very sensible. He asked the Man, "Is this Buster?" When the Man admitted it, Norman or Lord Tebbit said, "I think he's had a worse

118

press than he deserves. He ought to hire a publicist to improve his image."

March 1, 1997

Another visit to Paws U Like by him and another profound embarrassment for me. This morning he went to buy a bag of sawdust balls and came home with Lumineck, a fluorescent collar which glows yellowy-white in the dark. I am to wear it when we go out at night so as to be clearly visible. On our evening walks we never leave the pavement. So the collar can only be protection against cars which mount the curb and threaten to cut me down as I sniff my way along the footpath. But he still put it on before we went out at eleven o'clock.

Sometimes I think he has no idea of the traumas he causes me. The blood of tundra wolves runs through my veins. My instinct is to stalk my prey, silent and unseen. How can I live out my destiny if I have an illuminated neck? He thinks it all a great joke. "Dog collar," he cried, giggling. "It looks like a proper dog collar. The Reverend Doctor Buster." I thought of nights in Siberia, baying at the moon and waiting to rip out the throat of an unwary traveler.

March 14, 1997—Sheffield

I wonder what tea tastes like. I only drink water and had never thought of it until the Man's mother wanted to give me some this afternoon. But I have thought of it ever since she poured some into her saucer this afternoon. "Buster doesn't drink tea," the Man said. "Don't you listen to the vet?" she demanded. "The vet recommends a saucer of tea every day." The Man did not look up from his newspaper. "Mine doesn't," he said. I could see that his mother was getting angry, and I lay down behind the sofa. But the Man didn't seem to notice her change of mood. "You go to Mr. Newton, don't you?" his mother asked. She seemed to know the answer already. "Mr. Newton is the one who told me that dogs should have a saucer of tea every day. If he told me, why didn't he tell you? He said it was good for dogs' coats."

"His coat looks all right to me," the Man said, with total justification. Indeed, most people regard my coat as absolutely magnificent. One young lady asked if I had highlights put in at the hairdresser's. Even his mother could not claim that it was capable of improvement, so she said, "Don't be silly. I didn't mean him. I meant dogs in general. I give Sally a saucer every afternoon." It hasn't done much for her coat. She looks like a moth-eaten goat. I do not need tea, but I would still like to know what it tastes like.

March 22, 1997—London

When I bit the Man today, it caused me far more pain than it caused him. His hand didn't even bleed, but I was deeply wounded by what the incident revealed about his understanding of my character. After more than a year of close friendship, he still seems confused about the difference between dogs and people.

As usual, in the early evening, I was sleeping on the sofa, occasionally stretching my back legs just for the pleasure of hearing him say, "Don't push, Buster." Then I began to dream. I dream a lot, though I seldom remember what I dream about. The Man pretends he knows. I am often woken up by his shouting, "Look,

Buster's chasing rabbits in his sleep. Look, you can see him running after them." I take no notice and doze off again as soon as he has quietened down.

But this evening I had a bad dream. A pointer had stolen my rawhide bone and a greyhound was sleeping in my bed. Twenty giant cats were chasing me down Victoria Street and a ghostly goose was whispering in my ear that it would haunt me for ever. Naturally, I whimpered a bit. Who wouldn't in the circumstances?

Stupidly, the Man leant down and, patting me on the head, said something he hoped would be encouraging. Although the patting had disturbed me, I was still half asleep. But I think he said, "You're all right, Buster. You're home with me." At the time it was just the noise that went with the blow to my head. Thanks to my reflexes—which are like a coiled spring—I had turned and snapped before I was fully conscious. I had never heard the Man howl before.

As soon as he had made sure he was not bleeding and he would not have to go to the vet, the Man said he forgave me. All She said is that it proved that I could never sleep on the bottom of the bed. I did not know the idea had ever been discussed. Now I think about it, I am very much in favor.

Tolerance

March 17, 1997

My communications crisis has deepened. I have developed a huge repertoire of endearing noises. Each one of them has a precise meaning—time to go out, I'm dying of hunger, I can't get the rubber bone from behind the desk and there ought to be room on the sofa for me. I do not expect him to hear high-pitched whistles. For he is no more a sheepdog than I am and I can't even hear his cell phone ring if it's in his inside pocket. He ought to take the trouble to understand what I say to him. But whatever question I ask or suggestion I make, he has two stock responses. He either accuses me of whining or denounces me for attention-seeking.

To make things worse, I am having increasing difficulty in understanding some words he says. When I barked at a man in the street this afternoon, he said, "Buster, I sometimes find your idiosyncrasies incomprehensible." When I almost strangled myself on my collar by leaping into the air in the hope of catching a pigeon, he told me, "I actually find something attractive in your mindless indomitability." Back home, he described our walk as "moderately satisfactory" and, turning to me, added, "But you will have to develop a little tolerance towards strangers. They aren't all intent on grievous bodily harm." What worries me is that, when he finds out I am only a dog, he will stop loving me.

April 4, 1997

I am only surprised that it has not happened before. This morning, as we were walking down Victoria Street, a young woman with obviously dyed hair turned round and said to the Man, "Who do you think you're talking to?" He was talking to me. But I am so low on the ground that some people do not see me. Sometimes I feel like the invisible man.

It was what the Man had said to me that made the young lady particularly keen to know if he was talking to her. As I recall, it went something like this, "For God's sake, walk properly. If you wobble about all over the pavement, nobody can get past." The Man answered the young lady's question by pointing at me. She went red, but said nothing.

The incident illustrates an important point. Being rude to me is regarded as funny. If he said the same things to other people—"Sit! . . . Lie down! . . . You'll go out!"—he would be in terrible trouble.

April 16, 1997

He has been away. He says he has been to Pakistan, but I do not believe him. If he had been abroad, he would still be in quarantine. Although he tells me lies, I miss him when he is away. Without him at home, there is no one for me to dominate.

I was on my evening walk when he got home. As soon as I got in, I could see him sitting in the study at the far end of the hall, and She let me off the lead straight away. I ran to greet him in a spirit of joyous welcome. Although I say it myself, I am a great jumper—four feet up in the air and ten feet along from a standing start. With the advantage of a run-up, I am like a ballistic missile with fur and teeth. The need for physical contact was so strong that I could not waste a minute before I started to chew his hand. I longed for the old, familiar voice saying, "For God's sake stop it, Buster, or you'll go out." So I took off from just outside the study door.

If the Man had not lost his nerve, everything would have been fine. But he held up his arm and tried to duck behind it. Instead of my landing neatly on his knee—as I certainly would have done, had he not panicked—I bounced off his hand and ended in a heap on the floor. A less agile dog would have been badly injured. Fortunately, I managed to twist in the air, so at least I landed right-side up. But as I flew through the air, my paw caught him a glancing blow on the cheek.

I have drawn blood for the first time in a year, and the damage was done—by mistake—to my best friend in all the world. I think I am being corrupted by civilization.

April 24, 1997—Derbyshire

Derbyshire is full of strange animals. Some of them are very small. When it rains very hard and water runs down the hill, little green things jump up and down. I caught one in mid-air. It was cold and slimy. I spat it out straight away. Little brown animals stick themselves to the wall at the bottom of the rockery. They smell quite nice, but when I got one in my mouth, it was hard on one side and wet and slimy on the other. I began to think all the little animals in Derbyshire are wet and slimy somewhere. But they are not. There are small things that fly about which are hard to catch, but I was clever enough to get one. It buzzed about inside my mouth, so I spat that out too.

Coming home last night, I smelt an animal next to the water trough where the Man tries to make me wash my feet when it is muddy in the fields. I went to get a closer sniff and it pricked me on the nose. Every time I pushed it to make it stop, it pricked me some more. I think it must have had prickles sticking out all over. The prickles made my nose bleed. The Man was very unsympathetic. He said, "You were trying to roll that hedgehog over so you could kill it." That was not true. But it was a good idea. I shall know what to do next time.

April 28, 1997—London

Exile from St. James's Park has proved less of a punishment than I anticipated. I have not been there for a year and do not miss it. I miss the geese, but I would not mind never seeing a flamingo or a pelican ever again. Flamingos are a sickly pink color and pelicans have buckets where their beaks ought to be. I can't bear anything unnatural. Birds should be brown or black with, at very most, a touch of red or silver on breast or wing. And they should have something sharp at the front of their faces. I now regret that I got a goose instead of one of those weirdoes.

But the great thing about Green Park is the effect it has on the Man. Now that he has convinced himself I won't commit suicide by throwing myself under a bus in Piccadilly, he is far more relaxed, and, since I reflect his moods, I am too. In St. James's I was weighed down with the responsibility of convincing him that the walk would not end in catastrophe. So, apart from the one goose, I behaved very well. In fact, in general I behaved better than he did. It was not me who said to the park keeper, "If you try to kick my dog again, I shall kick you and I won't miss. He was only trying to look in your wheelbarrow."

In Green Park I run about in a way which I pride myself is both uninhibited and responsible—never going too far away to hear his call, and eventually responding to it. Self-respect requires that I take my time. He didn't want a Sealyham or a dachshund, so he must not expect me to behave like one. And since he boasts to his friends that I am "a dog of character," he ought to rejoice when I prove him right in Green Park.

There is, however, one disadvantage to our new route. We approach the park across the front of Buckingham Palace, where the Queen lives. The Queen must be one of the Man's best friends, because we always have to be on our very best behavior when we go past her house. If I so much as pause by the wall or railings, he yanks the lead so hard that my collar almost takes my head off. Then he winds the lead so tightly round his hand that I have to walk close up against him. He says, "Come on, Buster! Light infantry pace." He always says that when he is agitated. All I can think of is how to avoid him standing on my paws, but he goes on about what will happen if I try to bite anyone.

This morning, even though we went past Buckingham Palace very early, the road outside was crowded with people. I think they were Japanese. They usually are. They are pack animals like dogs. They hunt in groups, each one led by a lady who holds an umbrella up in the air, whether it is raining or not. They always look at us as if they have never before seen a man and dog fastened together by a piece of string. This morning, one of them pointed his camera at me and made a big flash. When I barked the Man told me, "They eat dogs in Japan. If you do that again, I shall let them take you home for breakfast." I did not believe he would do it. But just to think of such a thing reveals a distressingly vicious streak in his character.

May 2, 1997

For the first time in my life I have been left alone all night. They both went out as soon as I had had my last walk and did not come back again until after breakfast-time today. They thought that I did not realize they had gone. Stupidly they forgot about my fifth sense—since they don't have much of it themselves. Perhaps I ought to have been pleased that for once I could sleep free from the smell of humans. But I felt very lonely.

When he came back, the Man was very tired but happy. He kept saying having Norman Tebbit there all night made victory all the sweeter. Can this be the

Norman or Lord Tebbit that we met in the park? And, wherever they spent the night, did Norman or Lord Tebbit take his dogs with him? The Man kept saying, "We have waited for this for eighteen years." I shan't mind if it's another eighteen before they leave me on my own again.

May 6, 1997

The Man says Green Park has gone to my head. All the running with Silky, Sandy, Cliquot and Lenny is supposed to use up my energy. But on the way home today I had some left over. So when I saw a young lady dancing along in a way which made her arms wave about, I danced along beside her. I was still on the short lead, so it wasn't easy, but I managed to get a little friendly nip at her sleeve.

"Look what your dog's done," she said to the Man. "It's torn my sleeve." It was not a very big tear. "Has he done that?" the Man asked, as if he hadn't seen me do it. "It's only fun, you know. It's his way of being friendly." That was true. But the young lady did not seem to think it made up for having her sleeve torn. "I will pay for it," the Man said and she gave us her address. She turned out to be a neighbor, but I do not think the Man wants to see her again.

The Man talked about the young lady most of the way home. "I don't think she's the sort who would go to the police. But you never know. Better give her enough to keep her happy." Then he said to me, "More training for you, my lad. We'll have to have Steve round again. More discipline." Then he groaned. I think he dislikes discipline more than I do.

PART V

Realization

In which Buster begins to rediscover life's harsh
reality and, briefly, feels grateful for his good fortune,
before relapsing into some of his old bad ways.

May 8, 1997—London

When the Man got home last night, he took his coat off
and went into one of those strange routines which
make me doubt his sanity. Tired though I was, I tried to
gratify his whim. The usual ritual involves an oddly
shaped piece of red rubber which he calls a
bone—though it does not resemble any bone I have
ever chewed. For reasons I cannot imagine, he enjoys
throwing it to the far end of the hall. Crying "Fetch it!"
and "Quickly! Quickly!" he then waves in the direction
of the point on the carpet where the "bone" landed.

Usually I humor him by behaving like a retriever—
which I am certainly not. But then he throws the

"bone" down the hall again and expects me to go through the whole routine once more. Being human, he is profoundly cynical. So he assumes that I pander to his strange tastes because I get a biscuit as a reward for running about with a foul-tasting piece of rubber in my mouth. In fact, it is my contribution to the Care in the Community organization.

The "bone" ritual being over, I am expected to do what, in his vulgar way, he describes as "give him a cuddle" on the sofa. This requires me to sit next to him and, when he pretends not to be looking, suddenly lick his face. Actually, as long as I am not too tired, I do not mind it very much. Face-licking is natural to me. It is how young wolves tell their parents they are hungry and invite them to regurgitate some unwanted food. And I have not quite forgotten my primitive roots. But he never regurgitates unwanted food. So I slide down onto his knee and sleep as soundly as I can with him fidgeting about with the television remote control. Through my dreams I can hear him talking about devotion.

Realization

May 10, 1997

I thought at first that Steve from Blue Cross was my friend, because he said that when I did something right I should be rewarded with a biscuit. Now I am not so sure. This afternoon, he brought the Man a book. There was a drawing of a dog on the cover and, in big letters, the words DOG-TRAINING FOLDER. Beneath the drawing of the dog it said, "This folder belongs to . . ." The Man wrote "Buster." Steve said, "You'll have to treat it seriously or we'll get nowhere."

Pages one and two were about old stuff—the rules which I resent but accept with dignity and don't need to be rubbed in. "The family eat their food first. . . . The family clear away after eating. . . . Your dog is then fed." The quality of the advice can be judged from rule three. "No food to be given to your dog by anyone while they are eating." If Blue Cross can't get the grammar right, their views on dog-training are unlikely to amount to much. But I am reconciled to mealtime tyranny. I was not, however, prepared for section two. It was called "Ignore the Dog," and the title page was illustrated with a drawing of a neglected puppy and a woman who was too fat to be an advertisement for mealtime discipline.

The next pages said, "No touching. No looking. No talking"—all the things that make a dog's life worthwhile. "When your dog demands attention in any way from anybody, they [same mistake again] must completely ignore it. If your dog keeps demanding, turn away, stand up or leave the room." There was then a list of all the things I most like to do. "Using the paw. Nudging with its muzzle. Staring at people. Barking, whimpering, whining. Stealing items and running off with them. Body-slamming people. Mouthing, nipping, biting. Putting its head on laps." Body-slamming is my favorite. I am not supposed to do any of them.

It then said, "This seems harsh, cruel and can be an emotional strain, but the reward of a better-behaved dog is worth the effort." Worth it for whom? Certainly not for me.

May 17, 1997

We have been in the park every morning this week and Silky was nowhere to be seen. Nobody—not Lenny,

Cliquot or Sandy—knows what has happened to her. They think she is all right because her owner is a nice man and will look after her. But we are all afraid she has moved to another town.

The Man says I shall forget her quite quickly, as my memory is very bad. That is, in a way, true. I do not think of Silky when we are at home. But when we are in the park, I wonder why there is nobody to jump on me. I am a creature of habit. One of my habits used to be running headlong at Silky and knocking her over. Cliquot and Lenny are too low down to knock over, and Sandy spends most of his time in the air, jumping after his stupid rubber ring.

May 24, 1997—Derbyshire

In the afternoon we went into the village of Bakewell to get more sawdust balls—"for dogs with a tendency to put on weight." I was not allowed into the pet shop. When the Man came out, instead of complaining about how much I cost to keep, as I had expected, he said, "Buster, you'll never believe what I've just seen. There is a dog in there which is almost as tall as

Barley and even heavier." He looked so surprised that I believed him.

Barley is the Irish wolfhound in our village. He is so big that he can lean his elbows on a six-foot wall. As far as I know he has never jumped over it. I can jump over any wall I can lean my elbows on. Barley is, no doubt, too big to be athletic. That is why I would not like to be in his collar.

I would not like to be the big dog at Bakewell either. If what the Man says is true, he sits in a little room of his own and never moves. This is not because the pet-shop owner is unkind. It is because the dog, which is called Tchaikovsky, is only a puppy (fourteen months old) and his legs are not strong enough to bear his weight. He weighs two hundred pounds, and in a year, will weigh two hundred twenty-five. By then, his legs will be strong enough for him to go on walks.

Tchaikovsky is a Saint Bernard, which means he has bloodshot eyes and several double chins. When the pet-shop owner came out to the car with a sack of sawdust balls, the Man asked him, "When Tchaikovsky grows up, will he have a brandy barrel hanging from his neck?" The pet-shop owner said, "Everybody asks that," and the Man stopped smiling.

Realization

June 10, 1997—London

We have changed the route by which we go to the park in the mornings. We still go past the offices of the Transport and General Workers' Union and he still says when I stop near the wall, "Go on, Buster. You do that to them, like they did it to me in 1976, during the Winter of Discontent." But we do not turn left between the two pubs with the tubs of flowers outside their doors. The Man has read in the *Evening Standard* diary that the pub owners are angry with me, and he does not want to meet them face to face.

On warm nights the pub owners' customers stand outside the pubs on the pavement. As well as making it difficult for people to walk past, they waste bits of perfectly good food by pushing it into the soil in the flower tubs. Naturally, when I walk past, I want to dig it up and eat it. Unfortunately, it is impossible to dig up the food without digging up the flowers. "I don't know how you do it so quickly," the Man said to me. He sounded really proud of me.

Buster's Diaries

June 18, 1997

I have discovered a new way to frighten the Man. It is called mad running. Mad running should not be confused with pointless running, at which I have been adept for some time. Mad running is more frenzied. Mad running is only possible when he and I are joined together by the long lead. This is how I do it. I walk demurely for some time. Then I suddenly set off at full speed and keep going until (this is a joke!) I am at the end of my tether. Then, without slowing down, I run round him in circles. This requires him a) quickly to change the lead from hand to hand, b) to rotate until he is dizzy, or c) to allow the lead to wind round him like cotton round a bobbin.

Whichever he chooses, he is pretty confused for a while. Before he has time to recover, I turn in from the circle, charge at him as fast as I can go, and leap in the air just before we collide. Sometimes I hit him, sometimes I don't. At first, he thought I had gone crazy. He pulled on the lead until he caught me and then began to calm me down by rubbing behind my ears and scratching my tummy. Sometimes he sinks to his knees on the wet grass so as to calm me better. Calming always included giving me a biscuit. I was sorry when he decided that it wasn't rabies after all.

Really, he ought to be flattered. I am treating him like another dog, which is what he pretends to like. If he had my powers of observation, he would have noticed that mad running and crazy jumping are exactly what I did in the park when Silky was there.

But mad running only frightens him. Mad running is not possible without getting tangled in the lead. As you turn in from the circle it goes slack, and if you have four legs to worry about, one of them is certain to get caught. He has seen it happen a hundred times. But he still thinks I shall break a leg and is even more frightened than he was when he thought I had periodic rabies. "Sit! Sit!" he shouts, in a way which is more likely to excite than to calm me. Then he unwraps me. And, of course, I get a biscuit. I told you mad running was fun.

July 1, 1997

I always knew that no good would come of the railings around Westminster School playing fields in Vincent

Square. As I could have told them, the grass has begun to grow over the concrete foundations—nature has always been more difficult to hold back than humans realize. However, until it really begins to spread across the path, I am put in constant danger.

I have never denied that I like a little grass from time to time—purely for medicinal purposes. But, unfortunately, grass is addictive. I begin to nibble at the end of the blade and I cannot stop myself until I am right down to the root. Before I realize what has happened, my head is through the railings and stuck. My natural instinct is to rotate my head sideways and come out sideways. But that only makes the problem worse. Naturally I panic.

The Man then says, in an infuriatingly calm way, "Nothing to worry about, Buster," and tries to turn me the right way round so that I can escape. It always feels as if he is trying to screw my head off, and I panic even more. I get out in the end, but not without badly bruised ears and a feeling of panic that puts me off the purpose of my lunchtime walk. I cannot wait for July when, with any luck, the grass will be right across the pavement again.

Realization

July 12, 1997—The Lake District

Against my better judgment, we are spending a weekend in the village of Troutbeck at the Staffordshire Bull Terrier Rescue Annual Walk and Charity Auction. He is here to help. I would be more impressed about his concern for dogs' welfare if he had not forgotten my food. This morning, I was only saved from cornflakes by the owner of our hotel, who sold him a bag of the inferior mixture he gives to his spaniel bitch. It tastes far worse than what I get at home. I doubt if this part of the trip will be mentioned in the article he is writing for *The Times*.

We went on "the walk." Actually we didn't. We joined the walkers about a mile along the route and led them up a little hill. As soon as the photographer had taken our picture, we walked back down again. He then went for lunch in a pub. I would have been perfectly happy sleeping on the backseat of the car, but he has read an article (always disastrous) which claimed that dogs in cars die of heat exhaustion. So I had to be under the table among the cigarette ends, with nothing to look forward to except the hope of him spilling his crisps. Fortunately, he is a messy eater, so something dropped down about every five minutes. I hate cheese and onion.

The bullterriers were uglier than I had imagined. I knew that they would look pretty grotesque. But as well as having muzzles squashed back into their skulls (as if they had all run head first into a brick wall), they were all bow-legged. I can't believe that my mother was like that. Dad, a handsome Alsatian, wouldn't have looked at her twice—even if she'd been dressed up in the fancy gear they were selling at this reunion.

Half the dogs had spikes in their collars. Some even had silver medallions dangling round their necks. That sort of kit was on sale at the charity auction. But he doesn't like that sort of thing. I fancied a Stars 'n' Bars kerchief tied under my neck to make a rebel's bandanna. But he didn't like that either. So it's back to the old flea collar.

Some of the dogs on the walk were what I shall call disadvantaged. One was disadvantaged by having only three legs. Another was a stroke victim and dragged one paw. He wore a shoe to prevent the pads being rubbed raw on the ground. There was a blind bitch with a bell hanging round her neck. When you think about it, the bell made no sense. Her problem was knowing when other dogs were approaching, not other dogs knowing that she was about. Humans are sometimes very stupid.

The other dogs made exhibitions of themselves at the charity auction by just sitting there, on knees or at feet, without making a sound. I became star of the afternoon by giving a loud yawn just as the Man began to speak. He paid twice as much as it was worth for a giant bag of dog biscuits. Just as I was looking forward to the bag bursting in the car on the way home, he gave it back to be auctioned again. One way and another, it was a thoroughly bad weekend.

July 24, 1997—Derbyshire

When we got to Derbyshire today there was a new gate across the path that joins the two little gardens. It was clear enough that it had been put there to keep me out of the best garden—the one from which I can hear and smell the Labrador in the kennel. So from now on I shall not be able either to tear a hole in the hedge or to howl to him through the branches.

I have retaliated by destroying the top lawn in the

other garden by doing what the Man calls "hand-brake turns." I found out how to do it when he gave me a ball to chase, but it can be done with a leaf or stick or even my own tail. The trick is to chase whatever you are chasing so hard that you run past it. Then you push out your front legs to stop yourself going too far. As well as stopping, you swerve round so you are facing whatever you are chasing. When I first did it, I thought that the Man would say, "Clever Buster." But he only said, "Look at the bloody skid marks in the grass. He's doing hand-brake turns." That is when I decided to go on doing them in retaliation for the gate.

When he was not about, I had a jump at the gate and, because I am such a good jumper, I got my front paws on the top. With practice, I think that I shall get over, though it may scrape my stomach a bit. It would be better all round if the gate were left open or removed altogether. Then I could resume my attempts to rescue the prisoner next door, and there would be no ugly wounds on either my stomach or the top lawn.

Realization

August 10, 1997

Apparently, there are four spots under my chin. I have not seen them myself, but whilst we were larking about on the sofa, the Man noticed them and went very serious. Spots are very dangerous—at least for dogs. He often has them and takes absolutely no notice. But the four that have grown on me caused him great concern.

The Man held my jaws together and pushed my head backwards so that he could get a better look. Having your jaws held together and your head pushed back is much worse than having spots. After staring at them for about five minutes, he went and got a tube of cream and smeared it all over the underside of my bottom jaw. That was very frustrating. The underside of my bottom jaw is one of the few parts of my body I cannot reach with my tongue.

After the cream had been on my chin for about ten minutes, I forgot all about it and went to have a friendly word with the Man. I think he had forgotten the cream too. He rubbed behind my ears in a way which makes me put my head on his knee. He was wearing a good suit and I think it was the sight of all the cream on his trouser leg that made him so angry with me. "Look, Buster," he said, "if you keep rubbing it off, I'll have to take you to the vet." The Man knows I do not like going to the vet because, whenever I do, I get a needle stuck in me. It was an unfair thing to say. As he knew very well, I was not rubbing the cream off. Like him, I had forgotten about it.

If the Man does take me to the vet, I cannot see much being done to cure my spots. I went to the vet last year with a spot on my bottom. That is when I was so frightened that I stood in the corner with my face towards the wall and tried to bite the vet when he wanted to lift me onto his table. I got so near to biting him that the vet wouldn't look at my bottom until the Man put a muzzle on me. The Man took me back after he had bought the Baskerville.

After the Man had persuaded me to wear the Baskerville, the vet looked at my bottom and said that the spot didn't matter. If I go to see him with my spots, he will have to examine the other end. Even though I have a muzzle—that is really what the Baskerville is, whatever the Man says—I won't be able to wear it while he looks at my chin. So I shall be able to bite him if I want to—which I probably will. I hope that either the cream cures the spots or the Man decides not to take them so seriously.

August 12, 1997—Scotland

We came to Edinburgh so that the Man could talk about his book. He talked about it in a big tent. He did not want me to hear what he said, but She persuaded him to let me sit with her at the back of the tent. It was very hot and I got very sleepy. When I began to snore, everybody laughed.

Today was supposed to be the start of our holiday. We have sailed to Mull. The voyage was horrific. When we got on the boat the Man was told I had to be left in the car or kept outside on the deck. The Man said we'd both stay in the car. But he was told I had to stay on my own. All the motor cars were to be left unlocked, and, while I could be trusted not to steal anything, the Man could not.

The Man said we would stand on deck. It rained very hard all the way and we got soaked. What made it worse was that the Man could see into the saloon and the cabins through the portholes. Everybody inside was dry and warm. They were also drinking tea.

When we got into port, all the warm and dry people in the cabins rushed ashore first. Some of them had dogs on leads. The Man said, "Never mind, Buster. The dogs were not supposed to be inside the saloons and the cabins. We did what was right." Doing what is right makes no sense to me if you also get wet.

August 15, 1997

There is a lot of water on Mull, not just round the edges, but all over. Wherever you go, there are little creeks and rivers. The water is there because it rains all the time. In fact, all that happens on Mull is rain. And we went out in it four times a day.

The Man didn't seem to mind, but he had a coat and a hat to put on. I got wet all over and had to be dried in the bathroom before I could go and lie down in the bedroom we all shared.

The owner of the hotel in which we stayed talked all the time about his gundogs, which he has trained to pick up birds after he has shot them—the birds not the dogs. He said his gundogs had soft mouths, whatever that may mean. I think they have soft heads. Otherwise they would have eaten the birds instead of bringing them back to the hotel owner.

The best part of the holiday was when the Man drove our car into a ditch. It did not make much of a bump, but it made the Man very angry and She laughed at him. When he got out of the car, he stepped into the water in the bottom of the ditch. Now he knows how I feel when I get wet several times a day.

August 20, 1997—London

I have perfected a new trick. It is called teeth-snapping. This is how I do it. I am sitting next to somebody who is taking no notice of me—feeling naturally annoyed that I am being ignored. First I pant a bit or give a little whine. When the person turns round to see what the noise is all about, I make a sudden lunge and bring my teeth together about an inch from the person's face. When my teeth come together, I sound more like an alligator than a dog. Nobody likes this trick except the Man, and me, and he is told he should not like it.

"You'll be sorry," She tells him, "if he takes your nose off by mistake." That is a silly thing to say. I don't make mistakes like that. If I took his nose off, it would be on purpose.

August 27, 1997—Brighton

We have been on a day trip to Brighton. While he did something called broadcasting, I slept on a bed in a hotel room which had been specially booked for me. After the broadcasting and the sleep, we went down to the sea. I hate sea. You walk along beside it and it suddenly jumps at you and wets your feet and legs.

The one good thing about the sea is the birds. There are lots of them and they fly very low. Even though I was on my long lead, I jumped and almost caught one. When we were all alone on a deserted bit of beach, the Man let me off the lead and I jumped at the birds for a long time. I did not catch one, but I am sure I would have done if he had not made me go with him to the railway station.

When he put my lead back on, he gave me two biscuits and said, "Buster, you're a marvel. You'll never catch one but you'll never give up. You don't know your own limitations. That's what I like about you." Sometimes I fear he does not love me for myself. I am just the dog that he knows he can never be.

September 14, 1997—London

All is sadness in Green Park. Sandy died yesterday while playing with the rubber ring he always carried in his mouth. We were in Derbyshire, so we did not see it happen. But everybody told us about it when we got to the park this morning. They all say it will not be the same without Sandy bouncing up and down.

Apparently he was behaving just as crazily as usual, jumping high into the air to catch the rubber ring whenever his owner threw it up for him. But after three or four jumps, instead of landing on his feet, he just collapsed into a heap. They told us he was still alive but unconscious.

A kindly policeman took him to the vet in a motor car. The vet said Sandy had suffered a brain hemorrhage. He would not die for days, but he would never regain consciousness and be able to go into the park to jump for his rubber ring. His owner agreed that he should be put down straight away. "Put down" is not a very nice way to describe it, but I am sure it was the right thing to do—even though Sandy's owner said that he would have four hours each day with nothing to do with his time. Dogs ought not to be kept in great pain because their sentimental owners are too self-indulgent to face the anguish of parting. We are all entitled to die in dignity. The Euthanasia Society ought to form a canine branch.

The Man says we are all sad because it reminds us that the same thing will happen to us one day—though he knows very well that I do not jump up in the air all the time to catch a rubber ring. I thought about what he said on the way home and, when I decided he was right, made up a little poem either in memory of Sandy or to help me feel better about dying one day.

Buster, are you grieving
Over Green Park trees unleaving?
It is the fate that we were born for.
Buster, it is yourself you mourn for.

I shall call the poem "Spring and Fall." Sandy did both those things just before he died.

I have also been thinking about what Sandy's owner said about now having four hours each day with nothing to do. Does that mean Sandy had four hours of walks? If so, that is twice as much as I have. I think life is very unfair. So, no doubt, does Sandy.

September 22, 1997

A man called Paul Simons has written a book about dogs during the war. One, an English pointer called Judy, was a Royal Navy mascot and, when her ship was sunk, she was captured by the Japanese. After the war was over Judy got a medal and barked on the radio to celebrate Britain's victory. In the prisoner-of-war camp, she kept a lookout for dangerous animals. The book does not say what she had to eat during her years as a prisoner. Since that is the most important question, it cannot be a very good book.

If I had been in the war, I would not have wanted to be shipwrecked and kept in a prison camp. I would have behaved like Rob the "paradog." Rob, a collie, was parachuted behind enemy lines twenty times. He wore a parachute harness which looked just like the Precious Cargo safety belt I wear in the motor car— only Precious Cargo looks better because it is bright red. When I travel to Derbyshire tomorrow, I shall pretend I am floating down into enemy-occupied territory, not stuck in a traffic jam on the motorway. A dog who is essentially heroic by nature, but rarely does anything more exciting than chase a squirrel up a tree, has to take refuge in fantasy from time to time.

September 24, 1997—Derbyshire

It was always agreed that we don't do tricks. No sit-up-and-beg. No lie-down-and-play-dead. No come-and-shake-hands. It was the Man who first talked about a dog's dignity. He says that for me to hold out my paw when he tells me to "Say hello, Buster" is no better than an elephant standing on a stool when its trainer cracks a whip. It makes no sense to me. But I am supposed to take notice of what he says, so I now feel as strongly about the subject as he does. No tricks.

However, we are getting dangerously near to

breaking the rule, and I don't know how to deal with the situation. On wet mornings, when we get back from the long morning walk, I have to be dried. To be honest, I rather like it. The Man gets a big, rough towel and rubs me all over—always being careful to stroke my fur in the right way. To be dried is to be the center of attention and that is what I like most.

The paws are the difficult part. The Man takes the paws very seriously in Derbyshire, where there is a lot of mud and, as he always says, I do not have the sense to keep out of it. The paws have to be rubbed clean, one by one. He is beginning to expect me to pick them up. "Come on, Buster," he says in his most ingratiating voice, "give me a paw." I have only to twitch in annoyance for him to shout, "Look! Look! Buster's picking his paw up when I tell him to."

How does picking up a front paw in order that it can be dried differ, trickwise, from shaking hands? The answer is: Not at all. It is another example of his double standards. And I can't help trying to do what he tells me. I get a biscuit every time one of my paws leaves the ground.

PART VI

Sophistication

In which Buster's horizons are widened by the discovery
of how other dogs live, and he comes to the conclusion that
collaboration is preferable to resistance.

October 2, 1997—London

The wolf inside is not quite dead. But earlier today, I wished he was, for he caused me very considerable embarrassment. I was walking through Mayfair when She stopped at a shop called Farloe's.

Although my memory is not good, it can be swiftly jogged by a sight, sound or smell. In Farloe's window, there was a hedgehog—one of those animals with spikes on the outside that made my nose bleed last year.

Naturally, I tried to get it and roll it over like the Man had suggested after last year's unprovoked attack. So I pounced. Fortunately, my head is very hard and I did not hurt myself on the glass. Although She was pulling very hard on the lead, I would have pounced again, but a total stranger spoke to me. He said, "Don't be silly, Buster. It isn't a real hedgehog. It's a boot cleaner."

I was pleased to be recognized by somebody I had never met before. But I felt very silly making such a mistake. I must try to keep my instinct in check until I have found out what is really going on.

October 9, 1997

The scales fall from my eyes! Last night, when we went for our late-night walk, Barley the Irish wolfhound and Biggest Dog in the World was asleep by the glass door in the side of his house. He was all curled up with a woolly toy. I think it was a rabbit.

Being a romantic at heart, I have always imagined Barley hounding wolves in Ireland. But he sleeps with a woolly toy! I shall attack him the next time that I see him in the street.

October 13, 1997—Derbyshire

We have fires in Derbyshire, and the Man is very proud

of his fireplaces because they are so old. Sometimes he is very proud of things because they are so new. It is often very difficult to follow his reasoning.

Fires have flames which come from coal and logs. The coal comes every Saturday on a truck. An English bullterrier puppy sits on top of the coal. He is called Dennis, and the coalman says that he is pure white. When we see him sitting on the coal at the back of the truck, he is pure black. Dennis is very well behaved. He never jumps off the truck, even when it is driving along, and when it stops outside our house, he lies down on top of the sacks and waits for the coalman to make his delivery. I give him a bark nevertheless, just in case he is tempted to trespass on my territory.

The Man asked how Dennis is washed clean at night. The answer was difficult for me to believe. The coalman said they go into the shower together. Showers are rooms in which water comes out of the ceiling. I hate going out in the rain. Making it rain in a room inside the house seems crazy to me. But the Man seems impressed by Dennis's story. I fear the worst. Within a day or two he will be dragging me into the shower.

Buster's Diaries

October 19, 1997

The Man's pyromania, which has come between us ever since he bought the house in Derbyshire, almost gave me a heart attack last night—far worse than the normal bother we have when he lays a fire.

Usually the trouble comes about because I try to help. It always annoys him, even when I don't get distracted by the logs. Some of them have most interesting smells and a few are edible. He always gets bad-tempered when I take them out of the basket, especially if I run into the ashes that he has scraped out from the grate. After I do that, I always get sent outside—even though it was an accident, and running through the ashes doesn't matter any more because they are spread all over the carpet.

Being put outside means I miss the best bit of making fires. When the coal and the sticks and the logs have all been piled up, he sets them alight. I always wag my tail when I smell the smoke and he is always gratuitously offensive. "Stupid dog would burn himself to death if we let him. Hasn't the sense to know that fire burns." He then puts a steel thing across the front of the fireplace to stop me getting anywhere near, and I have nothing to do except to sleep on the sofa or sit in the window and defend the property from attack by barking at whoever goes past. Last night, however, his passion for fire nearly caused a major rift in our relationship.

I at least was ready for bed. The Man—who washes in a basin instead of licking his own hands and feet—takes much longer. So, having had my last walk, I was waiting for lights-out, when I was suddenly sent into the kitchen and the door closed behind me. "I don't want you tripping me up on the stairs," the Man said. I haven't tripped him up on the stairs for months, but he is often unfair about such things.

As soon as I was let out, I went to bed in my upstairs basket right against the radiator. Strangely enough, I am allowed to lie with my tail touching the radiator, but I am forbidden to go anywhere near the fire. Another example of the Man's inconsistency. But he has managed to convince me that fire is dangerous.

I remembered what he had taught me when, at about two o'clock in the morning, I smelt smoke coming from under his bedroom door. Cometh the hour, cometh the dog. So I did my duty and barked a warning. But he did not wake. So I ran across the land-ing and up the half-flight of stairs which leads to his forbidden bedroom. My barking still did not wake him. He would make a terrible guard dog. So I scratched as hard as I could on the door—even when bits of paint and splinters of wood got stuck between my claws.

At one minute I thought I heard a muffled shout. It sounded almost like "Go back to bed, Buster, and quieten down." But, fearing it was a cry for help, I barked and scratched on. Dogs have been awarded medals for less.

Exhausted from my efforts, I fell momentarily into a half-sleep. But as soon as I awoke I resumed the rescue attempt. Believe me, becoming Dog of the Year was the last thing on my mind. All I wanted was for the Man—and my regular supply of sawdust balls—to be safe. When he opened the bedroom door, I was so over-joyed to see him that, after one quick jump at his head—not easy from halfway up a flight of stairs—I forgot all my training and ran past him into the bed-room. A fire was burning in the little grate.

For the first time in months, he let me sit on the bed. "It's all right," he said. "I'm not burning to death or suffocating." You see, he has begun to read my mind. "I brought it up in a bucket while you were locked in the kitchen. Thought it looked nice." Then he got very sen-timental. "Were you looking after me? Did you think I'd

get burnt to death? What a good boy." It was late, I had
endured a disturbed night, and he was rubbing behind
my ears. Naturally I went to sleep, proud and contented.

Suddenly I felt a tug at my collar and I bounded
off the bed, ready for another act of daring self-sacri-
fice. The Man spoke to me in his most authoritative
voice: "Out you go and back to bed. And no more barking. Even if you don't need a good night's sleep, I do."

October 26, 1997—London

Returning from Derbyshire today, I almost had a nasty
accident—more proof, I fear, of the importance of
putting my rambunctious past behind me.

Throughout the journey, I was the very model of
reticence and restraint. In short, I slept from start to
finish. The Man did not wake me up until we were
alongside the St. Pancras railway station platform. So I
barely had time to stretch.

When the Man got off the train, I made the mistake of jumping out of the carriage at the same time,
instead of waiting—as I am supposed to do—and fol-
lowing obediently behind.

I lost my footing and my hind legs slipped off the platform. All that stopped me from falling under the (fortunately stationary) train was the power of my front legs and the lead round my neck. The Man hauled me onto the platform, and said, "Buster, you'll give me a heart attack one day."

It should have been my heart attack that he was worried about. Once again, I have been reminded of the advantages of denying my instinct to leap first and look afterwards. Oh, how all occasions do inform against me!

November 2, 1997

I have just seen a picture of a dog in yesterday's *Times*. It was called Zuki, and looked to me like a Great Dane. It was hard to be sure because he (or she) was leaning on his (or her) elbows at the edge of a swimming bath and was wearing a bathing cap to keep the water out of his (or her) ears. Thank God I don't swim. If I did, the Man would certainly buy me a bathing cap and I would look as ridiculous as Zuki.

Zuki's picture illustrated a whole article about keeping water out of dogs' ears. The vet who wrote it says that wet ears never cause healthy dogs a problem. "A well-groomed dog runs with ears flapping like butterfly wings." I do no such thing and I pride myself on my grooming. Particularly my ears.

November 5, 1997—Fireworks Night, Derbyshire

The Man spent all evening making me feel nervous. I am not sure what he expected to happen, but he drew the curtains and blinds all over the house and made me sit with him on the sofa. He even brought my water bowl into the sitting room, something he has never done before.

About every thirty seconds he repeated, "There is nothing to worry about, Buster. You're all right with me." The television was on so loud that I could barely hear him, but, after he had said the same thing ten times, I could guess what he was saying. When She told him he had promised to go to the doctor about being deaf, he got very bad-tempered and shouted, "You know very well that it's to stop Buster being frightened."

We all had to stay up—with the curtains drawn and the television on—until very late. When we went to bed, the bangs which I could just hear over the noise in the sitting room had stopped. I had been looking forward to listening to them all evening.

November 9, 1997—London

Today, I invented Buster's Ratchet—no relation to Buster's Collar, the ridiculous lampshade which dogs with conjunctivitis wear round their necks to stop them scratching their eyes. Buster's Ratchet is a new form of psychological warfare to be employed in the historic conflict between dog and man. I am barred from entering the most interesting rooms—largely, I suspect, because those are the rooms in which the Man takes his trousers off. He does not seem to like me jumping at him when he is naked.

Unfortunately, those rooms are the places in which he spends his time when I am waiting to go out in the morning. Sometimes I think his behavior is designed to provoke me. For as soon as he wakes up, he asks me, "Want to go for a walk?" Of course I do. And I am ready. But he is not. It takes him forty-five minutes to prepare for a stroll in the park.

At first I am perfectly happy rolling about on my

back and growling aimlessly. "Joy of living," he calls it in his sentimental way. But after about ten minutes of banging my head on the skirting board and getting carpet fluff up my nostrils, "joy of living" begins to lose its charm. And he is still not ready. A less sophisticated dog would run amok. I operate Buster's Ratchet.

First I lie, motionless, just outside the bedroom door. "Now, Buster," the Man says, "you know perfectly well you are not allowed in here." Then he turns round and I wriggle two inches forward. He turns his back on me and says, "That's a good boy. Stay there." So I wait and then wriggle another two inches towards him. By the time he is ready, I am more inside the bedroom than out. It doesn't make him move any more quickly, but I have won the war of wills and taken another step towards undisputed leadership status.

November 30, 1997

One of the many bits and pieces which came with today's *Sunday Telegraph* had a picture of something called an Italian greyhound on the cover. The Italian greyhound was called Vinny and it got into the newspapers by going—or, more likely, being taken—to see a dog psychologist. Apparently Vinny is afraid of men. I found it all embarrassing, but the Man thought it very funny. "Don't look so superior, Buster," he said. "There are those who think you are a psychotic killer." He knows very well that, in the affair of the goose, I only did what comes naturally. He just can't avoid making sick jokes about it.

In fact, most things Vinny did were perfectly normal. When his owner (a lady, you will not be surprised to learn) sat with her boyfriend on the sofa, he forced himself between them. In a motor car, he climbed on the driver. I guess that the "animal behaviorist" charged for his advice. I would have told them what was wrong with Vinny for absolutely nothing. The lady owner actually boasted, "My father and Vinny have dinner together every night—that is to say, my father cuts up some of his own meat and vegetables and gives it to him." The most elementary dog book warns against feeding dogs from your own plate. Whenever I suggest it, I get hit with a newspaper. Anybody who knows anything about dogs realizes that, if dogs eat with humans, they begin to think of humans as inferiors. Perhaps it is best to live with somebody who knows absolutely nothing about dogs.

December 4, 1997

We have invented a brilliant new game called "Get the pig's ear." The ear the Man and I chase is not attached to a pig. It was once, but the pig died and its ear was cut off and dried. It is very good to eat, but first it has to be chased round the room.

The Man gets one out of the cupboard, waves it about and then throws it down the hall. I pounce, but I do not chew it or swallow it down. Instead, I let it drop out of my mouth and stand with it between my front paws. Although the Man is not always highly perceptive, he realizes after a little while that I am challenging him to get it back.

Every time he moves a muscle—a pace to the right or a slight wave of the left arm—I run off with the pig's ear. Sometimes I go into the kitchen and sometimes round the furniture in the drawing room. After a minute or so, I bring it back and challenge the Man again.

The Man is a bad sport. He always catches me and

gets the pig's ear in the end. Then, when he has made me sit down calmly, he lets me eat it. He is trying to show who is boss, but he also proves which one of us is really stupid. "You'd make a rotten tennis player, Buster," he tells me. "You do all the running about and I just stand here." Why does he not understand that I am not a tennis player? I am a dog and we do not play tennis. We play get the pig's ear.

December 10, 1997—Derbyshire

The central heating has broken down and the Man cannot keep the fire alight in his bedroom. He wasted most of the evening pushing bits of wood under the coal but, after a quick flare, it went out every time.

Just before midnight, he put two more blankets on his bed. Then he put on two sweaters over his pyjamas and the socks he had just taken off. "Bedtime, Buster," he said. I obeyed at once—as I always do. But instead of going to my night bed on the landing (next to the cold radiator), I went to my day bed in the kitchen (next to the warm stove).

The Man was offended. "Well, thanks for standing

by me," he said. Who does he think I am? I think the decision to choose the warm bed shows I am becoming positively sophisticated. He should welcome me becoming as selfish as a human being.

December 23, 1997—London

Silky and I are reunited. She was back in the park this morning. At first I did not recognize her. She is at least twice as big as she was when last I saw her. And her ears are now so long that they almost reach the ground. I think her owner must have read the article in *The Times* about ears flapping like butterfly wings. No risk of "bacterial growth" for Silky. All the bacteria would be battered to death against the side of her head.

Despite her new size and shape, we still have a lot in common. She has developed the dangerous habit of running about with a branch in her mouth. It mows down everybody on each side of her, like the blades on Boadicea's chariot wheels. But she dropped it as soon as she saw me and ran at me straight away. Both of us have retained our sense of timing. We went up on our back legs, clashed heads, fell to the ground and rolled about on the grass, all in perfect unison and just like old times. The other dogs—Lenny, Cliquot and the spaniel with a piece of rope tied to its collar—all watched in envy. Silky has lost her looks, but beauty is only fur deep. It is character and companionship that really matter, not appearance. The Man knows that very well. Why else should I love him despite him talking so much nonsense?

On the way home, he asked me, "What about Flora?" and then said, "Frailty, thy name is Buster." I have no idea what he was talking about.

December 25, 1997—Derbyshire

It is our good fortune to be spending Christmas with Sally and the Man's mother. I was not allowed into the dining room when they ate the turkey. Sally was. But a greater indignity followed. "How old did you say he was?" the Man's mother asked. "About three," he told her. "We guess he was born in January or February 1995." His mother seemed doubtful. "Did they tell you that at the place you got him?" The Man told her that they did. "They saw you coming," the Man's mother said—whatever that may mean.

The Man insisted that I must be three, but, thinking that his mother believed me to be younger, added, "I know he still behaves like a puppy sometimes." I think he was remembering the young lady from Yorkshire Television who, after I tried to sit on her knee, asked the Man, "Is he weaned yet?" The Man told his mother he was glad I had not grown up, but that is not what he said to the young lady from Yorkshire Television.

"He's no puppy," the Man's mother said. "And he isn't three either. He's ten or eleven." Although it was Christmas, the Man said, "Don't be daft, Mum. You saw him two years ago. He's almost twice the size he was when we got him." That is not true, but I have grown. The Man's mother was not convinced. "He's going white under the chin. That's a sure sign of age," she insisted. She then went on about how sad the Man would be when he lost me in a couple of years' time. The Man tried to tell her my chin had always been white, like the patch on my chest. "It's part of his Staffordshire inheritance," he said. I think his mother went to sleep while he was talking about my handsome brindle coat, but I cannot be sure, because I went to sleep first. When I woke, I remembered what the Man's mother had said. For a moment I thought that it might be true. Then I remembered that I am young and bold. I am glad. The Man couldn't manage without me.

December 28, 1997

Great day. There is a picture of me on the front of the *Sunday Times* News Review. It is a good picture. My ears are pricked and it is clear that I have an Alsatian's profile. I am part of the New Year quiz. Readers have to guess my name. It must be a very easy quiz because everybody knows me. I am regularly mentioned in newspapers.

This is the second competition in which I have featured. The first one was in the *New Statesman*. They reprinted the old picture of me licking the Man's face—the one that the *Evening Standard* used on the day the Man was prosecuted for letting me kill the goose. Competitors had to invent a caption to put under my picture. I do not know what the winning contestant wrote. I hope it was "Good boy, Buster. Have a biscuit."

Sophistication

You can't trust David Attenborough. Before he went to bed, the Man sat me down on the sofa to watch a television show about wolves. I can't focus on the screen—though I sometimes bark when a door bell rings in *Coronation Street*. So the Man promised to repeat all the interesting bits. At first it was very good: "Wolves are more familiar to us than we might imagine. All our domestic dogs are descended from them. Indeed, the very characteristics we admire most in our dogs—loyalty, intelligence and courage—are precisely the characteristics that the wolf has to have to survive."

I know I look like a young wolf—cuddly in a frightening sort of way. And I have no intention of becoming one of those scraggy, unkempt geriatrics that slink along behind the pack, waiting to pick up bits of food nobody else wants. I like eating food nobody else wants, but it is a luxury, not a necessity. And the Man brushes me—not as often as he pretends, but quite often.

Anyway, when he told me about "loyalty, intelligence and courage," I rolled over on my back and kicked my legs in the air—though which of the desir-

181

able characteristics that illustrated, I am not certain. Indeed I felt so happy that I began gently to chew his finger. Inevitably, he went through the whole performance. "Stop it. . . . Bad dog. . . . Nobody likes teeth except Buster. . . . I shan't tell you again. . . . You'll go outside." As always, when I am euphoric, I chewed on and waited to be told to go. Indeed, I could feel him stirring in preparation for my stern expulsion when the Man sank back on the sofa. "Listen to this," he said.

"Did you hear that?" he asked, knowing very well that I hadn't. "He says wolves always pick on a wounded prey. Not very nice, is it?" I panted and gave my affectionate growl, hoping he would forget both about Attenborough's libel and about turning me out of the room. "It's right," he said, as if he had just made a major discovery. "It's another characteristic you've inherited from your primitive ancestors."

Epilogue

This morning, on the train down from Derbyshire, the woman who sat across the aisle from the Man pointed at me and said, "It looks as though he has fallen on his feet." I hadn't fallen anywhere, I was lying quietly under the table, chewing a pig's ear and waiting for the Man to unscrew the top from the bottle of water he had bought for me. The Man had just told her about me being an orphan and living in two dogs' homes before he adopted me. When I rolled back on my side and closed my eyes, the woman said, "He's as good as gold."

That is, I am glad to say, a bit of an exaggeration. I still bark at people who stop the Man in the street, jump on his knee without invitation, chew his hand when he lets it dangle down beside his chair and get bad-tempered when anything distracts him from his principal duty—paying attention to me. But I have become civilized almost to the point of decadence. Two years ago, I was wild by nature and had to force myself to behave properly. Now I am domesticated and need to be reminded of the wolf that sleeps inside me. The change of character may not be particularly heroic, but it is certainly convenient. It means that almost everybody loves me.

My greatest fans are two little girls who live near us in London. The one who is eighteen months old runs away from her mother and rings our door bell just for the pleasure of hearing me speak—even though she has to stand on tiptoe to reach the bell. I stand on tiptoe on the other side of the door and bark in my most friendly way. When she looks through the mail slot, she can see my tail wagging. I can hardly believe that, a year ago, I would have wanted to drive her away.

Her father has bought her a machine which the Man calls a virtual pet. Its name is Tamagotchi, but the little girl calls it Buster after me. I am sure that it will grow up to be very well behaved.

I think I would have learnt more quickly if, from the very beginning, I had been brought up like the two little girls. As far as I can make out, they never lived rough in a park or got moved from orphanage to orphanage with nobody to talk to them. I only remember that it happened to me because the Man keeps telling people about it. To be honest, I don't remember much, unless a smell or sound reminds me. And these days all the smells and sounds are warm and comfortable.

The End